JACK AT THE GATE
A Jack of All Trades novel

DH Smith

Earlham Books

Published 2018 by Earlham Books
Book design & cover art by Lia at Free Your Words
(*www.FreeYourWords.com*)

Text copyright © 2018 DH Smith

ISBN: 978-1-909804-32-6

PART ONE:
A CELLO AND A HOTEL

Chapter 1

Jack pushed back the step-ladder and the bucket to make room for the cello case on the grubby sheets. His daughter Mia was behind him scowling. She was in her school uniform, her backpack bulging with books. Jack slammed the side door of the van shut.

'Keep it there,' she hissed, kicking the van tyre.

'Easy on my van. What's it ever done to you?' He was rubbing his hands together on a frosty morning. 'How'd that happen?'

He'd spotted a long scratch in the *Jack of All Trades* motif painted on the van. He ran his finger along the scratch. Some kid with a coin maybe.

'Nobody'll notice,' shrugged Mia, 'with all the dirt and stuff.'

He had to admit she had a point, what with flecks of sand here and there, grime picked up from the road. Still, the van was running and that was what mattered. It was his mobile tool shed, running ad, rain shelter and lunch hut.

'Get in,' said Jack, 'while I clear the windscreen.'

He scraped off the frost with a scraper that was a freebie from a builders' merchant. It had been a cold night, and the ice resisted the scraper, but persistence won. He straightened a side mirror, spat on it and wiped it with his sleeve. Hardly worth cleaning the back window; he could hardly see out of it with all the gear in the back.

Jack climbed inside and belted up.

'I want to give up the cello,' said Mia.

Jack turned the engine on. It caught first time. Good. He'd let it run for half a minute to warm up. He sat back, thinking ahead about the digger and skip that were coming.

Half attending to his daughter, he said, 'Why?'

She blew out her cheeks. 'It's a dumb instrument. Takes ages to learn to play decently. Then you've got to perform with other people.'

'Why's that a problem? Aren't you a team player?'

Still engrossed in the digger for the coming job, half listening. He couldn't do anything unless it was there. He rubbed his hands together. The van took ages to warm up in this weather, his hands were still wet from scraping the window.

'You don't know anything,' she exclaimed.

Full attention on her now. Cellos and other people, she'd said. Something like.

'I'm sure any instrument can be played by itself,' he said carefully. That seemed sensible to his limited musical brain.

Mia rolled her eyes. 'Sure, you can play the cymbals by themselves, or a trombone for that matter.' She sighed wearily. 'A cello is an orchestral instrument.'

'Right,' he said, nodding in agreement as if he'd known that all along. 'Don't you want to be in an orchestra?'

'Grade 3 orchestras are crap.'

He hesitated, trying to fathom what she meant. Ah yes, her music exam.

'You'll get better.'

She thumped back in her seat. 'I don't want to get better. You try carrying a cello on your back in the morning. Getting on a full bus. All the dirty looks you get as you bash people. Squeezing it between pushchairs and old ladies…'

'I wish I'd learnt an instrument at school.'

'You're welcome to it.'

He took off the handbrake, glanced in his mirror and headed off.

'I saw a small group with a cello in it once. What do they call it?'

'Quartet,' she said with a shrug.

'Yes,' he recalled. 'A posh do. I remember bits of nosh on sticks. Two blokes, two women, all in black playing. Two violins as well. One bigger than the other.'

'That was a viola,' she said.

'Like a family,' he said. 'Baby violin, teenage viola, mummy cello and thump thump thump, daddy. What's it called, the big one? In jazz bands.'

'Double bass.' She blew out her cheeks. 'I wouldn't mind playing in a jazz band. But you never see a cello in a jazz band.' Her shoulders were slumped, she'd pulled her feet onto the seat. 'All the music I get is classical music. Nothing fun, nothing you can dance to.'

A cyclist was coming towards him. He slowed to give her space, the road too slippery on an icy morning. He wouldn't like Mia cycling on days like this.

'You could be the first jazz cello,' he said as he gently accelerated.

'That's just what Mum said.'

He laughed. Him and Alison in agreement made a change. Mostly they argued, a pattern they'd got into, forced to communicate because they had a child to bring up.

'It's a lovely looking instrument,' he said. He admired the wood of it, the curves, a most female instrument.

'You don't have to carry it,' she said. 'On your back. And practising all those boring scales and arpeggios until you are sick to death of them.'

An arpeggio sounded like a variety of pasta. But clearly his daughter wasn't in the mood for jokes. He'd had no music at secondary school, not much of anything, as he hadn't been there much.

'You have to stick at things,' he said, wishing someone had held him to it. Five years of secondary school and he

3

hadn't even turned up for the final exams. A waste of every-body's time, his English teacher had said. All he'd learnt was how to shoplift and drink. No certificates for that.

'I'd like to play the guitar,' she said. 'You can sing along to it. There's electric and acoustic. And it doesn't weigh a ton.'

'I'll talk to your mum,' he said.

A car was coming towards him down the narrow road. He or it had to give way, as there was no space for his vehicle with cars parked on both sides. He stopped, the car ahead stopped. Jack would have sworn but Mia was with him. He signalled for the car to back up and pull over. The car signalled for him to. But there was a car behind Jack so he couldn't. No room.

He sighed and opened the van door.

'Keep your temper,' hissed Mia.

He nodded. Good advice. This wasn't worth a fight. Keep calm. The driver of the car had also got out. They walked towards each other, breath showing up in the cold air. The man was stocky, buttoned up in a thick, dark grey coat to his knees, wearing a black woolly hat with a white bobble.

He said, 'You're taking up all the road. You gotta move over.'

'You're joking,' said Jack, gesturing at the lack of space. 'There's hardly room for a bike.'

'You move or I'll move you.'

The man squared his shoulders. Jack reckoned he did weights, was a wrestler or boxer. This was all he needed. What was up with the guy?

'I'd move if I could,' said Jack, holding up his hands to indicate he wasn't being difficult. 'I don't want to be stuck here. You could move into that space.' He pointed it out.

The man glared at him and brought up a fist. Jack was ready to evade the punch. This was dumb. A vehicle behind hooted.

'Look, man,' he said, 'You can knock me down. But that won't move my van.'

The man half withdrew his fist as if to reflect. Though Jack thought he still might deliver a punch for Auld Lang Syne. So as not to lose face.

'I've my daughter with me,' he said. 'I don't want any trouble. Short of a lift from a helicopter, I can't move forward or back.'

'I know you,' said the man, his eyes screwed up. He flicked his fingers. 'Jack Bell. Cumberland school.'

'A dump,' said Jack.

The man laughed.

'Tosser Potter!' exclaimed Jack, waving a finger at him in recognition.

'Don't call me Tosser.'

Jack took the warning. 'Johnny Potter. Didn't you have a West Ham trial?'

'Got me, Jack.' Potter slapped him on the shoulder. 'I'll back up.' He started back to his car. 'Must go for a drink sometime, mate.'

Jack didn't say, no thanks as he didn't drink, or that he had no wish to revive their relationship. A concession beat a broken nose.

'Yeh, up the Goldengrove,' he called as Tosser Potter got in his car.

Jack returned to his van. Potter's car drew alongside. He waved as he came past, Jack waved back.

'Who's that?' said Mia.

'A nasty little creep,' he said. 'I went to school with him. A bully and a thief. There was a gang of them at Cumberland.' He sucked his lower lip. 'What would he have done if he hadn't recognised me?'

'What do you think?'

'Smacked me one, because I was in his way. You wonder how people like him stay alive. Anyway, let's get you to school.'

He drove on, stopping at the main road. It was busy, he'd have to inch his way into the line of traffic.

'I was thinking,' said Mia as she put on her gloves and scarf. 'You could tell Mum cello practice is interfering with my schoolwork.'

He yelled at her, thumping the dashboard. 'How many arguments am I going to have this damned morning?' A hand slapped to his head, as he pulled himself back. 'Sorry. Tosser Potter set me off. All this traffic. I've got a digger coming. And you do go on, Mia.'

'I hate the cello.'

There was a splinter of space in the stream, barely enough, but he nosed out, a car hooted, but had to let him in. Jack gave him a wave and a smile, the man gave him two fingers.

'And I hate the rush hour.'

He turned down the side road by the school and stopped, putting on his hand brake.

'Now off you go. Have a good day. I'll see you at the weekend. Maybe we can get the telescope out. Be quick, I'm blocking traffic. I must be at work to make sure the digger's come.'

'Okay, Dad. Thanks for the lift.'

She was out and away, slamming the door. And a quick wave, as she went in the school gate, quickly lost amongst the other girls. A car hooted behind him, Jack cursed at the rush hour, the world so bad tempered and quick to react. Get out of it, get to work.

Chapter 2

As Jack drove up to The Gate Hotel, the skip was being dropped off in the drive from the back of a truck. The crane had almost lowered it to the ground where it trembled on the chains. A little way up the drive, like an expectant grasshopper, was the mini digger. Bob had left it as he'd promised. Good old Bob, he'd delivered. Alongside the monsters carving out motorways, it was a toy. But fine for this job, it would save his back, and you didn't need to go on a course to handle it.

He stopped in the driveway and put his head out of the window.

'That skip's for me, mate.'

'It'll be collected tomorrow,' said the driver. 'Don't over-fill it. I know what you guys are like.'

Jack didn't reply, and left the driver to finish the drop. The Gate Hotel was a large double-fronted Victorian house with a pillared portico. Where there had been a garage was now a drive through into the back garden which had become the hotel car park. There were five cars there as Jack drove in and parked.

He walked back, through the tunnel of the once-garage, just in time to see the truck driving off. Skip and mini digger both here. Work could begin, although it would be something of a hassle. The digging was out the back, but the skip was at the front. That was because there was no possibility of getting the skip through the arch. So Jack would have to cart out the soil on the digger. Time consuming, but it couldn't be helped.

Jack had borrowed the digger once before, long enough ago for him to forget what lever did what. So a refresher to begin with. The ignition key he found under the caterpillar tread where Bob had said he'd leave it. Same machine, older, with signs of hard use. A dirty orange with the paint peeling in places, making his van look clean in comparison. Over the top, in front, was the long arm, like the neck of a goose, with the bucket at the end like a nodding head.

It didn't have a cab, just a seat behind the engine and a few stick controls. It was a mini digger, for small jobs like gardens and driveways, not a heavy duty mammoth. He settled in the seat. The height was OK. The machine had only one speed, slow, and two gears, forward and back. That was the easy bit. Digging was trickier, bending and swinging the arm, working the bucket. It'd come back with practice.

Which began at once, as he needed to bring down the arm to halfway, to get the digger through the archway. After some trial and error, when he was glad no one was watching, he got the arm to the right height and drove the digger through, past the parked cars to the area of lawn where he was working. It was close by the house, the fire escape at one end.

It was flattering to call the scrap of ground a lawn. A scrubby bit of grass, lightly frost covered, with more earth than grass. Who'd want to sit out here anyway? Though there were two plastic chairs by the French window with a tubular ashtray between them. Cigarette ends were scattered about, as if the need to get the next lit up was too important to spare time to bin the last.

Jack's job was to make the grass patch into a parking area for two cars. To do that, Jack would have to dig out soil, level the ground, lay ballast as a base, then sand, and the concrete over the top.

He'd get the hang of the digger before someone came out. If he was going to hit a wall he'd prefer to do it unobserved. Jack went to his van and put on ear protectors, squashed against his woolly hat. The machine made a racket, shaking through his bones, the small engine overworked. Over the next quarter of an hour, Jack got the feel of the controls, recalling what he'd known nine months earlier when he'd last used the digger.

Enough play, time to earn money. There was a foot of soil to be dug out. The machine was well oiled, and the teeth of the digger bucket went easily under the soil and filled with turf and soil. He set off to dump the load. Past the cars, halting at the arch where he had to lower the arm a foot, then through it, and to the skip. Almost touching the sides with the machine, he tipped the bucket at the end of the arm, dropping the load into the skip.

Triumphant, he waved an arm in victory as if he'd just scored a goal. He stretched forward and patted the engine, like a pet dog having brought back a stick, and christened the machine Betelgeuse, after the red giant in Orion, on the grounds that orange was almost red. And the digger might yet be a giant when it grew up.

He worked on, taking out the soil loads. The frost remained on the grass but hadn't penetrated far enough to affect the digging. The work, though, was cold, he was simply pulling levers. No heating or cab on this machine. Although he had on fingerless gloves, his fingertips were going blue, the chill penetrating his overalls. He'd work as long as he could take it, then warm up in his van, heater on and thermos of coffee.

Two men came out through the French windows holding hands. They sat on the plastic chairs, close together, legs stretched out and watching Jack as one of them lit a cigarette. He was surprised they could stand the racket of the machine, it was bad enough for him, through the ear protectors. Then again, this was a pre-work cigarette; they wouldn't be here long enough to be deafened and frozen.

But it wasn't a regular gasper; Jack was familiar with the smell of cannabis, confirmed by their faces settling into grins as they took in the smoke, passing on the spliff and giggling.

Both were middle aged in suits, one thin and tall, the other a portly black man. Jack was the spectator sport. They made the odd remark as they passed the joint, which Jack couldn't hear, shouting into each other's ear. Jack was gratified they hadn't come out half an hour earlier when he was at the bottom of his learning curve. They touched each other, nudged each other's legs, handed over the spliff like a love token.

Jack was returning from the skip, when a youngish woman came through the French windows with steaming mugs on a tray. He'd pulled onto the grass to get his next load when she yelled above the din.

'I've a coffee for you, Jack.'

He turned off the engine, surprised she knew his name, but of course – his van.

'I'll leave you a fortune in my will,' he said, taking the steaming mug from her, caressing the warmth.

She smiled through perfect teeth. She was mixed race, a light teak complexion, her hair in a scarf, like Rosie the riveter, except she was slimmer and wearing a housecoat rather than overalls.

'There's sugar,' she said indicating the tray.

She passed the other coffees round and Jack took three teaspoons of sugar. Normally he wouldn't, but this weather screamed calories. The two slices of toast he'd had for breakfast were ancient history.

'Jack of All Trades,' she mused, indicating his van.

'That's me.' Wondering if she had a smart reply. Someone usually had.

'And master of none!' exclaimed the tall thin man, chuckling as if he had created the greatest joke since time began.

'At least you know who I am,' he countered, 'and you won't forget me.'

'Interesting branding,' ruminated the portly black man. He held out his hand to Jack, which Jack shook. 'Clem James. I'm off to a marketing conference on graphic design. I'll bring you up, Jack. Your branding. Is it more positive than negative? Discuss.' He chuckled and took the spliff.

'Good as a name badge,' said the woman, joining the discussion. 'But so so as a reference.' She held a placatory hand up. 'But don't let me criticise. What do I know?'

'You know how to fry an egg and make crispy bacon,' chortled the tall thin man as his breath and the smoke mingled.

The woman turned to Jack. 'Fi. Should be Fi Dogsbody. Cleaning, cooking, general information, scrambled eggs and bedsheets. That's me in a nutshell.'

'Pleased to meet you, Ms Scrambled Egg.'

She laughed. 'As it happens, I've a breakfast left over. Ordered last night, and then she skipped off without paying. The boss is hopping mad. But it's in the oven and I'll only have to throw it out. These guys have just eaten, so do you want it?'

'With pleasure.'

'Come into the kitchen.' She indicated inside with her head.

'Hey! You're taking away our entertainment,' exclaimed Clem.

'Smoking weed is bad for you,' she said with a school-marmy wave of her forefinger and a mock stern pout as she went through the French windows.

Jack followed, coming into a large sitting room-cum-diner. The near half had a sofa and two armchairs in front of a large TV. The other half had three small tables with chairs which had been cleared of crockery. Just sauce pots remained.

'Eat in the kitchen,' she said, taking him into a side room.

The kitchen had a wooden table in the centre, a six-burner range, with pots and pans dangling from hooks that came off a high bar attached to three walls.

Fi placed Jack at the table and took the food out of the oven with oven gloves. She put it down in front of him.

'Ms Fly-by-Night had the cheek to order two eggs, sausages, bacon, beans, toast, marmalade and coffee for eight o'clock on the nail,' she said as she handed him a knife and fork. 'And then she hops off with the lark. I heard her go out. I came in at 6. But thought nothing of it, I've enough to do, what with cleaning and breakfast.'

'Early start you have,' said Jack as he began eating. 'What time do you finish?'

'Ten o'clock.'

'My God, that's a long day.'

'Ten o'clock in the morning,' she said with her perfect smile. 'I'm an actor. You know, resting most of the time. Some rest! I work here six days a week. Make the breakfasts, do as much cleaning as I can fit in, and then I'm off to do my own thing.'

'Which is?'

'I go to auditions. A waste of time most of them. I look through *The Stage*, phone my agent, wait for the phone to ring. You know, usual stuff. I'm rehearsing a lunchtime play at the moment. No money in it. Keeps my hand in, a TV producer might come in. Who knows?' She shrugged. 'Keeps my CV warm.' She snapped her fingers. 'Talking of warm, there's some cold toast I was about to throw out. Do you want it?'

'Please,' he said. 'I so need this.' Indicating the full English in front of him.

An Asian man came in, short and wiry, mid 30s, wearing grey trousers and a bright white shirt open at the collar.

'Are you spoiling our builder, Fi?'

'It would just go to waste, Malik. It's been in the oven for the woman who did a runner.'

Malik threw up his hands. 'I should have suspected it when she came in without luggage. She said the airline were sending it on today. I should have said money in advance.'

'Why didn't you?' she said.

'Stupid. That's why,' said Malik. He laughed outrageously as if it was a huge joke and sat on the table. 'You won't get that every day, Jack. My misfortune is your luck.'

'He's a secret millionaire,' said Fi.

'I wish, I wish. Would I still be here?' He got off the table and swung his arms around. 'This dump? I have business men cheating their employers by staying here on the cheap, two whores in and out like the birds in a cuckoo clock, dope-head queers, a single parent with two kids. And guests who do a runner first thing.'

Not a lot of respect for his guests, thought Jack. Though he was hardly in a position to pull him up. This was the guy employing him, not Mia.

'He makes pots of money,' went on Fi.

Malik was swinging his arms as if to indicate his poverty, looking here and there to find it.

'She thinks I'm coining it in, Jack. She doesn't consider overheads, the repairs, the inspections. Thinks it's all profit. I wish, I wish.'

'If I had a tenth of your money, I'd retire,' exclaimed Fi as she put dirty crockery in the dishwasher.

Jack realised this was an everyday joke. Warmed up each morning, but at least they got on, there being bosses and bosses.

'I've got another job for you, Jack. Finish your food, I'll be back in ten minutes.' He flicked his fingers and turned to Fi. 'I can't go to the theatre with you tonight.' He rolled his eyes and pointed upwards with a finger. 'Her upstairs.' He took a screwed up ticket from his pocket. 'You have it.' And placed it on the table in front of Jack.

'Hey, you can't do that!' exclaimed Fi. 'I gave it to you.'

'And I gave it to Jack.'

'I didn't give it to you to give away.'

'Got anyone else to go with?'

'No. Not at the last minute.'

'Now you have. He's a good looking guy. I'm fixing you up. Keep it, Jack.'

Jack looked from one to the other nervously, and said, 'You can't do that, Mr Bashir.'

'Malik. Anyone who says Mr Bashir, I look around and wonder who they're talking to.'

'She doesn't necessarily want to go to the theatre with me,' said Jack.

'She – who's she?' declared Fi. 'The cat's mother?'

'I just mean it's not down to Mr Bashir, er Malik,' he said, 'to decide who goes to the theatre with you.'

'Quite right,' she said, folding her arms.

Malik threw his hands up. 'You two argue about it. All I can say is I can't go. Family argument. I have to take Geela to see her sister.' He strode to the door and turned. 'Back in ten minutes, Jack. Don't rush. Talk to you about the job then. Meanwhile, the famous soap star Fi Morton can entertain you.'

And he was gone.

Jack crunched toast into his scrambled egg. The theatre ticket lay on the table. He was uncomfortable, having been pushed by Malik to take it. Fi was certainly attractive, but she wasn't offering the ticket and he wasn't going to push it.

'Don't feel you have to,' he said. 'It's your ticket, not mine.'

'He's a troublemaker,' said Fi pursing her lips. 'Delights in it.' She began wiping the counters, spray in one hand as she went along with the cloth in the other.

'Are you famous?' said Jack, taking a forkful of eggy beans.

She guffawed. 'Three weeks in *EastEnders*. Then I was murdered. You know the way it is? They don't murder stars, not often anyway, so they bring on a newcomer, build her up. Then kill her off. I got recognised on the street for about a month, earned more in those three weeks than I did for the rest of the year. But I came down to earth soon enough. My next job was an ugly sister in the panto at the Hackney Empire.'

'You're not ugly, if you don't mind me saying so?'

She laughed. 'Flattery will get you anywhere. Or at least a theatre ticket, if you want. Don't feel you have to. But I ugly up well. A straggly wig, a huge false nose, spots on the face, long shoes and a waddly strut.' She put on a posh squeaky voice, her hands on both hips. 'Get a move on, Cinders, enough scrubbing of the front step. You've a thousand sequins to sew on my ball gown.'

Jack grinned. 'What a bully!'

'Not a flea's bite on Geela.' She pointed up top. 'Malik's missus, throws her weight about and does sod-all.'

'While you scrub and clean and wait for Prince Charming to bring the glass slipper.'

She scoffed. 'That small feet fetish is highly suspect. Not that a prince will ever get near The Gate Hotel. Cheapskate place.' She was wiping the oven top. 'Keep your princes. I want to make it as an actor and take my pick of what's on offer. In the meantime, I'll wipe down cookers, make beds, and pick up spliffs and throw them in the bin. I don't weep by the fire.' She stopped working, the cloth and spray in her hands. 'I said, you can have the ticket. Do you want it? I was given two free. My friend's in it. Come if you want. I'm not forcing you. I know not everyone likes theatre. Do you know the King's Head?'

'That's a pub up Islington, isn't it?'

'About half a mile down from the Angel. Yes.'

'I don't drink,' he said hesitantly.

'I'm not exactly dipso myself, having to be up at five in the morning. Say yes or no? Be decisive. It's make your mind up time.'

'Yes. And thank you.'

'I've no idea what it'll be like. Could be brilliant, could be rubbish.'

'I'll chance it. Bit of culture will impress my ex.'

'Meet me seven thirty at the King's Head.' She threw down her cloth. 'Put your dirty dishes in the sink. I've got to change some sheets.'

And she swept out of the room.

Jack finished his breakfast. He could do with a cup of tea. Dare he make himself one? Best not. It wouldn't do to take advantage. There was a teapot on the side. He felt it, still warm. He poured himself a cuppa. Somewhat stewed, but he'd had worse.

He was adding milk when his phone rang.

Alison. What did she want?

'Hello, Alison.'

'You've got Mia's cello.'

It hit him. He could picture her leaving, waving amongst the schoolgirls. No cello.

'It's in my van,' he said. Had to be, as he hadn't got it out.

'What on earth is it doing in your van? Mia needs it, or let's say she did need it for her music lesson half an hour ago.'

'She said it was this afternoon.'

'I don't care what she said. Why is the cello in your van?'

'She forgot it.'

'And you forgot it too.'

'Yes.' There was no point arguing, though he frequently did as she wound him up so tight.

'The cello teacher has agreed to an extra afternoon lesson. Can you get the cello there?'

'Yes.'

'Get it there then.'

She rang off. Alison was used to giving orders, a head teacher in a primary school. But she wouldn't talk to her staff like she spoke to him. Or did she? Could she really order them around like school kids? Or was it reserved for her ex? He shook a fist at the hanging pots.

Control yourself, count twenty backwards. And get the cello to the school.

Chapter 3

'Thanks for breakfast, Malik.'

'It's nothing,' he said, flapping the gratitude away. 'Like Fi said, it would have just gone to waste. The woman did a runner, and ordered breakfast too. Would you believe it!'

They were in the hallway, up from the main door. At the desk, which had barely room behind it for a chair, Malik was straightening leaflets for activities and shows.

'Never mind. The trials of a hotel manager. She's gone. Forget it. Move on. There's some work upstairs in room 6 that I want you to quote me for. Making a big room into two small rooms.'

'Let's have a look at it,' said Jack. Not giving anything away before the job was seen.

Malik spotted something on the floor and bent to his knees.

'Katya with her shoes. Look! Like knives.' He was rubbing the carpet with his fingers. 'See what they do. And here and here,' indicating dents in the floorboards. 'You can't win in this place. Damage all the time. All makes work for builders – eh?' He rose and nudged Jack in the ribs. 'Do you like it that I set you up with Fi?'

'I'm meeting her at the theatre,' he said awkwardly. 'Let's see how it goes.'

Malik rubbed his hands together. 'I should run a marriage bureau. Instead of this doss house of a hotel.'

'Slow down,' insisted Jack. 'I've only known her twenty minutes.'

'You could do worse, my friend.' He laughed, wagging a finger. 'I tell you this, she won't be on the market forever. Fi works hard, she could be a star, earning a fortune.'

'And I could be Taylor Woodrow, and you could be running the London Hilton.'

That pleased Malik no end. He was shaking with laughter. 'This hotel would fit into one of their grand suites.'

Their attention was caught by a woman clumping down the stairs clinging to the banister. She wore ultra high heels, a leather skirt above her knees and fishnet tights on thin legs. She had a full bosom, too big it seemed for the slight body it was attached to. Behind her was a man, attempting to shield himself from their gaze.

'Hello, Malik,' she said. 'I hope you are well this morning.'

She spoke precisely in an Eastern European accent which Jack couldn't identify. Not Polish as he'd worked with a Pole a year or so back. Her teeth were yellow, almost matching her lank, blonde hair, cut almost like a swimming cap. She was heavily made up, the lipstick pasted on as if she were on stage; an older woman trying to play the romantic lead. The man behind her had his head down; Jack glimpsed a grey suit and shiny black shoes.

'Good morning, Katya,' said Malik. 'You didn't go out about six thirty this morning?'

'Me, up so early? I'd have to be crazy. I sleep when I can. I don't go for an early morning run. Leave that to the young girls.' She grinned, a ringed hand going to her face. 'I am a working girl, I need my beauty sleep.'

She laughed, stepping to the side, which left the man behind her exposed, but he reacted quickly to stay in her wake.

Jack noted her wrists, the veins and sinews showing through, the fingers almost skeletal, which made the fullness of her breasts a mismatch. They keep her warm, he thought, which she'd need in this weather.

Katya continued on her way, high stepping like a dressage horse, the man managing to work his way in front of her as she passed Jack and Malik, keeping her as a partial shield. The man quickly opened the door. Katya waved as she went through.

'See you soon, dear,' she called and closed the door.

'Too soon,' muttered Malik. 'I don't know how she does it. Must be 50, at least. And that man? Who does he think he's kidding? He's the vicar of St Jude's,' said Malik. 'I've seen him a dozen times.' He shrugged. 'But she always pays on time. Can beggars be choosers? Always polite, even when she's stoned. I tell you, it's an education, a hotel. All human life comes through. I did hear screaming last night, I'm sure. I was surprised, as Katya is considerate. She tidies up after herself. Though Fi moans about the used condoms she finds under the bed.'

'Hard to blame her.'

Malik shrugged. 'Hotel life. All tissues and stained sheets. You don't want to know what goes on. Let's go up.'

The staircase was wide, suggesting to Jack this had been quite a grand house. The green carpet was faded in the centre, almost a track. He noted some of the banister supports were loose. Traffic.

They came to a landing with numbered rooms on both sides.

'Do you live here?' asked Jack.

Malik shook his head. 'That would be a waste of money. Just an office upstairs. Geela and I alternate. Run the bar, I sleep upstairs in the office, open the door for latecomers. I was on duty last night. One here, one at home.' He nudged Jack. 'How to survive married life. Don't see too much of each other.' He laughed.

Jack didn't comment, it wasn't his place. If they alternated then they hardly slept together. A working relationship. It cut down on rows.

Malik stopped at a door numbered 6. He took out a key, and went to put it in the lock. He tried several times.

'That's strange. It's blocked.'

He looked nonplussed at Jack.

'Let me have a look.' Jack took the key from Malik and tried it in the lock. It went in part of the way, and was halted by an obstruction. He took out the key, got down on his knees and peered into the keyhole. 'There's something there. I think it's a key.'

'Can't be. The room's empty.'

'I don't know about that,' said Jack, 'but I reckon there's a key in there.'

'There can't be.'

Jack rose. 'Have a look.'

Malik got down and looked into the keyhole. 'Something there. I don't understand this. The room's empty.'

'Maybe it isn't,' said Jack.

'Someone is abusing me,' exclaimed Malik. 'This place!' He punched a fist into his palm. Then took a deep breath and knocked gently on the door. 'Hello in there,' he said politely. 'Hello. Can you open up for us, please.'

There was no reply.

'Either drunk,' said Malik, 'or keeping shtum.' He bit his lip. 'I will not be used like this. Can you get in without doing any damage?'

'Should I?' said Jack. 'If someone is still in there?'

'Dead drunk,' exclaimed Malik. 'Open it up. I need to sort this out. I don't know what's going on.'

'Let me get some tools.'

Jack went out to his van to root through his tools. There was the cello on his dirty cover sheets, accusing him, Alison's deputy. He had to get it to school by the afternoon.

Time enough. And he had to get back to the digging. Had the materials arrived? Before going back upstairs, he went out the front. Not there yet. But time enough. Plenty of digging yet.

Jack went in the hotel the front way, and up the stairs where he saw that Fi had joined Malik at the door. She was carrying clean sheets in her arms.

'It should be empty,' she said. 'Or at least, it hasn't been booked.'

'Someone let someone in,' growled Malik. 'And it wasn't me.'

'Couldn't have been me, could it?' said Fi, 'seeing I left here at 10 am yesterday.' She turned to Jack and rolled her eyes. 'Are we just going to stand here?'

'Knock on the door,' said Malik.

She sighed and handed Malik the sheets. Then rapped on the door, bolder than the earlier knocking. 'Hello?' she called loudly. 'Hello, whoever you are. You must let us in.'

Malik called out, 'Please don't cause trouble. Just open this door and then you can leave. No hassle. We won't try to stop you. But we need the room. Thank you.'

They waited. Malik had his ear to the door.

'Nothing,' he said.

'I'll knock the key through,' said Jack.

He'd brought a screwdriver, a six inch nail and a hammer to knock the key out, so Malik could use his key. He'd try the screwdriver first. He pushed it into the keyhole, as far as it would go. Then he tapped the head with the hammer. No movement. He hit the screwdriver head sharply. Then again.

'It's out,' he said, as the screwdriver went through and they heard the key tumble to the ground.

'Thank you, Jack,' said Malik. 'Let's see what's going on in there.' He put his key into the lock and turned. 'I hope we don't need that hammer,' he added with a half laugh. 'We should have card entry on these doors. I want it. But Geela says no. You see the problems we have? Guests always walking away with keys. Then what's to stop someone coming back for free?'

He turned the handle and pushed the door open. He stepped in, Jack and Fi followed.

The room was in semi-darkness. There was a smell of alcohol that carried him back three years. Waking up in rooms like this, head pounding and sick. He was pretty sure what they were about to find. Jack flipped the light switch. The light didn't go on.

'Something wrong with it,' said Fi. 'Never works. Guests have to use the standard lamps. You must get it fixed, Malik.'

'I will.'

'You always say that.'

'I will,' insisted Malik.

Fi had crossed the room and drew open the curtains on one of the two windows, grimacing at the alcohol stench. She rounded the double bed between the two windows and drew the other curtains. With the sun shining in, the room was in full view. It was large with the usual hotel furniture including two standard lamps, one by the bed, the other by an armchair and coffee table. There was a three drawer chest of drawers with a small TV on it. In the bed, a woman was out to the world with the green duvet to her chin, her face to one side on the pillow. A chair next to the bed had her clothes on, flat shoes on the floor under it. A handbag was on the armchair. No luggage, as Malik had said.

'It's the woman!' exclaimed Malik. 'The runaway. She didn't run away. Drunk, look at her.' He picked up an empty whisky bottle from the floor. 'What did I say? Alkies!' He threw up his hands. 'I bet she's wet the bed.'

'She was supposed to be in number 8,' said Fi. 'What's she doing in here?'

Fi was at the bedside and was feeling the woman's cheek. First one side then the other. She then put her hand in front of the woman's lips which were slightly parted. Fi turned to Malik and Jack.

'I think she's dead.' Fi felt the woman's neck, moving her fingers to feel the main artery. 'I can't feel any pulse. She's cold. Definitely dead.'

Fi stepped back, shaking. 'I didn't expect that. I feel quite dizzy.'

Jack led her to a chair. 'Sit down a moment.'

'Leave everything,' said Malik. 'I know what to do. I've had this before. A man had a heart attack last year in room 3. The ambulance came, we had the police too. They told me, don't touch anything just in case there's foul play.'

'She's not very old,' said Fi. '30s, maybe younger. So peaceful. Can it really be a heart attack? So young.'

'I had a cousin die at a rave,' said Jack. 'He was only 25. Drug induced heart attack.'

'Everyone out,' exclaimed Malik. 'I'm locking the room. I'll dial 999. It's their job now.'

Chapter 4

Jack went back to work. The woman was a complete stranger, but he was a little unnerved at finding her. Drunk. What demons had made her hit the poison? A reminder, if he ever needed reminders, of his sloshed days. The stupid anaesthetic. A cure worse than the illness.

He'd heard Malik on the phone to the emergency services, so it was all in official hands. All he'd done was knock the key through. Fi was more affected. She had touched the woman, searching for signs of life, had taken a longer look, felt her coldness. And maybe another woman, her age, was a reminder of her own death. Even so, she was a stranger to all of them.

He worked the mini digger, taking the loads out to the skip, endeavouring to keep the digging level and at the right depth. Jack was glad for the breakfast warm up, though he could have done without the added excitement, even if it was something to talk about. He berated himself for seeing the death as a topic of conversation. The woman was someone's daughter, someone's wife perhaps, maybe a mother.

He had just emptied Betelgeuse's bucket when the ambulance came into the driveway. Malik, who'd obviously been waiting for them, came out the front door. Jack caught some of what he was saying, about the woman who had died in the night. A car followed the ambulance and, in the passenger seat, Jack recognised his old friend, Fayyad.

Fayyad was always smartly dressed, today wearing a long, black coat, with black leather gloves, unbuttoned to reveal his suit, sky blue shirt and tie. He alighted with a tall, thin woman who went to the front door of the hotel.

Fayyad stopped by the digger. Jack turned it off.

'Fancy meeting you here, Jack. Do you know what's going on?'

'There's a woman dead upstairs. I was one of those that found her, but she's a complete stranger to me. Don't even know her name.'

'That's why we're here,' said Fayyad. 'Mr Bashir had her registered as Norma Jean.'

'Ah,' said Jack, recalling the name from pub quizzes when he did such things. 'Marilyn Monroe's real name.'

'Yes,' said Fayyad. 'And while it's possible the deceased has the same name, I doubt it.'

'So that's why you're here,' said Jack. 'Dead, under an assumed name. Bring on the detectives.'

Fayyad laughed. 'Got it in one.' He slapped his friend on the shoulder. 'Best get inside. Hayley is getting impatient.' He indicated the tall woman at the door, frowning. 'Let's see what we can find out about Norma Jean. Talk to you later.'

Fayyad joined his colleague and they entered the hotel. Jack had seen the woman before with Fayyad, distinctively slim and tall. Hadn't Fayyad told him she had a black belt in Judo?

He continued working, wondering if he'd be able to carry on much longer. There were medicos here, police, investig- ating the death of 'Norma Jean'. A woman who had given a fake name and was dead in the morning. How? Heart attack? Suicide? Surely not murder, she'd locked herself in, there was no blood. An empty bottle of whisky.

Alcoholic poisoning? He dismissed murder as too dramatic, just a way of improving the tale which he knew he'd be telling.

Ten minutes later, the policewoman came out to the workings and asked him to come into the lounge. She was wearing a navy blue dress-suit and flat shoes, having no need for the added height of heels. She was two inches over Jack without them.

'I've met you before,' he said. 'You and Fayyad are a team.'

'We get on well,' she said with a smile. 'Fayyad says he went to school with you.'

'We were at Cumberland School, same class. I bump into him every so often,' he said. 'I've been to see his family in Ilford a couple of times. One of the few from school I've kept in touch with.'

'I'm Hayley,' she said, then adding for the formality of the occasion, 'Detective Constable Hayley Amis, if you need to ask.'

Jack followed her into the lounge. Fayyad was there, seated on a wooden chair. On the sofa were Fi, Malik and an Asian woman in shalwar kameez. Katya, the working girl he'd seen earlier, was in an armchair texting on her phone.

'How long will this take?' said Fi. Her coat and shoulder bag were on her knees, she was plainly ready to leave. 'I finished work ten minutes ago. I've got a rehearsal in Covent Garden. I mustn't be late.'

'I won't keep you long,' said Fayyad. 'So let's start with you. You are?'

'Fiona Morton. I work here from 6 am to 10 am as cook-cum-chambermaid.'

'You found the woman, Fiona?'

'I went into room 6 with Jack and Malik. We couldn't get in at first, as the room was locked with the key in the lock on the inside. Jack had to knock the key out, so Malik could open up. I thought the woman was asleep at first glance, maybe drunk. There was a strong smell of booze. I was going to give her a shake. But she looked so pale. I felt her face and neck. She was cold and had no pulse. Obviously dead. Malik called 999.' She looked around to the others. 'I can't tell you any more. Can I go now?'

'One last point,' said Fayyad. 'Mr Bashir said you heard her leave early this morning.'

Fi gave a shrug. 'I thought I did. But obviously she hadn't gone. Someone left about 6 this morning. And as there was no one in room 8, we thought that she'd done a runner.'

Fayyad looked perplexed. 'She should have been in room 8?'

'Yes,' said Fi. 'Room 8 is a single room, and the woman came on her own. Room 6 is a double room. I went into room 8, thought she'd made the bed, some guests do that, and left. I should have realised the sheets were clean and there was nothing in the bin but I was half asleep.' She looked at her watch. 'There's nothing more I can add. I really must go.'

'So what was she doing in room 6?' said Fayyad.

Malik shrugged. 'The keys are the same for the two rooms.'

'But a strange mistake to make,' said Fayyad. 'If she's been given room 8, how did she end up in room 6, same key or not?'

'She was half drunk when she arrived,' said Malik. 'Room 6 is the closer of the two. She must've read the room number wrong. The key worked. The room was empty. So she took the room. A simple mistake.'

'Someone mentioned screaming in the night,' said Fayyad.

'I heard it,' said Katya. 'I thought it was a sex game. But not from my room.'

'Which room?'

Katya shrugged. 'I don't know. These walls are like cardboard. You can hear a fly sneeze.'

'Is that all from me?' pleaded Fi. 'I really must be at the rehearsal.'

'You can go, but I want DC Amis to look through your things.'

'Is that necessary?'

'The hotel is a crime scene,' said Fayyad. 'No one leaves this room without my say so.'

'Suppose the phone rings,' said the Asian woman, who Jack realised must be Mrs Bashir. 'Suppose a guest comes...'

'We'll deal with that when it happens.'

Jack said, 'There's nothing I can add. All I did was knock the key out. I went in the room – but you know that. Can I get back to work?'

'Sorry, Jack. But the whole hotel is a crime scene. Including the car park. You must stop work for the time being.'

'Can I use my van?'

'No, you can't.'

That was a double blow. Couldn't work, couldn't use his van. He had to wait on their timetable, and twiddle his thumbs in the meantime. Fi was by one of the small dining tables with DC Amis. The contents of her bag had been piled on the table. She was putting items from her pocket on the table too, obviously annoyed at the time it was taking and what she regarded as pettiness.

Jack said, 'There's a cello in the van that I've got to take to my daughter's school. Can I get it?'

'No, you can't.'

'It's only a cello,' said Jack. 'Surely...?'

'It's a crime scene, Jack. No exceptions. And if you want to leave, see DC Amis and give her your car keys.'

Jack was about to argue, but could see Fayyad's face was set. It would be futile. His friend was sticking to the rules and couldn't be seen to have favourites.

Chapter 5

The scene of crime people had arrived and been taken upstairs. There were too many unknowns around the death of the woman that warranted their presence. Fayyad was aware of the financial constraints. This could rebound on him. Scene of crime operatives were costly and could only be justified if something untoward had happened. Fayyad would have liked to search the other rooms, including the hotel office, but to do so, he would need a search warrant. And he didn't have enough evidence to justify it. It could be just an accidental death, but he had a feeling, compounded of experience and savvy, that something wasn't quite right.

He had to come up with something or he'd be torn off a strip by his boss for complicating matters. Spending money unnecessarily. Fayyad caught the doctor as he was leaving and spoke to him in the driveway.

'Would you oblige me with your first thoughts?' he said.

The doctor was middle-aged in a baggy grey suit, he wore a trilby to cover the last reef of greying hair.

'She wasn't hit on the head, stabbed or shot,' he said. 'But I dare say you've noted that yourself.'

'Is suicide possible?'

'Not likely. That would be a poison of some sort or an overdose. But for that there's usually a bottle, or tablet boxes, a glass, some sign of how it was administered. All there is is the whisky bottle. Possibly a heart attack, brought on by heavy drinking, but I can't confirm it. You'll have to wait for the autopsy. But I tell you this, there's considerable bruising on the woman, down her back and one side. I'd say she'd been kicked and punched recently.'

'Could that be a cause of death?'

'I don't think so, but I can't rule it out. Heart attack is my preliminary thought, but that's not definitive. Might be something else. Her organs need to be examined, blood tests. Sorry I can't be more helpful.'

Fayyad thanked him for his thoughts and returned to the lounge where Hayley was holding the fort. Katya had been allowed to go, but not to her room which annoyed her. But Hayley was a commanding gatekeeper.

Besides himself and Hayley, only Malik and Geela remained in the lounge.

'Would you please bring the guest book,' said Fayyad.

Malik went out into the hallway, to the desk, and returned quickly with the register. He opened it on a table. And the four of them stood round it.

'There,' said Malik. '11.20 last night. Norma Jean was booked in to room 8.'

'And the name didn't make you suspicious?'

'I'm not a film fan,' said Malik sheepishly. 'How was I to know?'

'She had no luggage.'

Malik shrugged. 'It happens. She told me she'd come from Heathrow and something had gone wrong with the flight. She said she'd be getting it tomorrow. Today that is.'

'Can we check this address, Hayley?' said Fayyad fingering the address written in the book.

'I'm already doing it,' she said, tapping into her smartphone. 'It's a Southend address. But that postcode doesn't exist. And there's no street of that name in Southend.'

'Double check,' said Fayyad.

'Can I go to the office?' said Geela. 'I'm no use here. I must do the accounts. VAT is late.'

'You can't,' said Fayyad. 'Unless you allow us to look through it first.'

'This is an outrage,' exclaimed Geela. 'This is not a police state. Why can't I go where I want to in my own hotel?'

'You know why,' said Fayyad.

'I shall report you to your superiors.'

'Here's my card,' said Fayyad, taking it out from his inside pocket and giving it to her.

'The office is private property,' said Malik.

Fayyad suspected dodgy bookkeeping. These small hotels. But that wasn't his concern, nor the obvious prostitute. Someone else's job, unless it related to the unknown woman.

'Please don't go to the office,' he said. 'Until I say so.'

He went back to the register, and looked down the columns. 'You had nine people staying last night. We'll need a photocopy of this page. We may need to question the guests.'

'Three of them have booked out,' said Malik.

'Which?'

'These.' He indicated the rows. 'See there? Paid, key returned.'

'I'm useless here,' exclaimed Geela. 'I've never met the woman, didn't book her in. I was at home last night.'

'Have you a witness for that?' said Fayyad.

'No. I was on my own. Watching TV.'

'You must both stay here in this room,' said Fayyad. 'Until the crime scene is vacated. One moment.' He went out into the hallway, and asked the uniformed police constable at the door to come in and to keep an eye on Mr and Mrs Bashir while he and Hayley went upstairs.

'Can you let me have the key to room 8?' said Fayyad.

'She never used it,' exclaimed Malik. 'It was empty last night.'

'Then there shouldn't be a problem letting me see it.'

'Give him the key,' said his wife. 'It makes no difference.'

Malik nodded and went out and shortly later returned with the key. Fayyad and Hayley left them in the company of the police constable. They went upstairs. At the landing they were given shoe covers and paper overalls by the officer standing guard. As they geared up, they could see into room 6 where the woman had been found, the door being open. Crime scene officers were at work, dusting for prints, taking photographs, a woman was on all fours checking the carpet.

The expense was worrying Fayyad. Could he justify it? He'd have to try. CSI were here and working. And if it were all for an accidental death... His boss would crucify him.

Hayley pointed out the door of the room up the corridor.

'Would you mistake a 6 for an 8?' she said.

'No. But then I don't drink.'

'You'd have to be almost paralytic,' said Hayley.

They went along the corridor to room 8. Fayyad opened up. The room was small with a single bed, and completely tidy. Fi had done her work, but then again, the room had not been occupied last night.

'Very basic,' said Hayley.

There was barely room for a dressing table and armchair along with the bed. A single wooden chair was by the bed with a table lamp on it. Coat hooks were on the door. No cupboards.

'She was booked to stay in this single room but somehow got an upgrade to a double,' said Fayyad. 'Was that by accident,' he added thoughtfully, 'or by design?'

'Malik Bashir booked her in,' said Hayley. 'I can certainly think of one reason why he'd give her a better room.'

Fayyad smiled slyly. 'That occurred to me. A single woman, on her own.'

'He might admit it if his wife wasn't present.'

'Maybe. But let's recap on what we've got. A woman comes here late at night, gives a false name and false address. The scene of crime officers say they have found nothing to identify her. No passport, no credit card. Explain that.'

'She had to leave in a hurry.'

'That fits with what the doctor said. He told me she's badly bruised. Punched or kicked.'

'Domestic violence? She could have run away from a violent partner.'

'Leaving without luggage,' went on Fayyad. 'Very little money in her handbag. Certainly not enough to pay for her room.'

'That could well account for her upgrade,' said Hayley. 'She did a deal.'

'Certainly points to it,' said Fayyad. 'Time for another chat with Malik.'

Chapter 6

Jack walked home. He was not in a rush; the crime scene people would be there for a few hours at least. And he couldn't work until they'd gone. Frustrating, but out of his control.

The day had warmed up, after the crisp frost of the morning. Just as well as he'd had to leave his jacket in the van. Along with the cello.

Alison would go bananas.

Was Fayyad being needlessly officious? Stopping him working, and even using his van.

Maybe not, he thought, trying to curb his resentment. An unknown woman had died in one of the hotel rooms. Until it was known how she died and who she was – it was best to keep everyone away. Difficult to argue with. Though he wanted to. They had to investigate, on the outside chance it was murder.

He couldn't have favoured treatment.

Jack was walking down Romford Road, a busy thorough-fare, traffic coming from the outer London boroughs and Essex, and jamming up through the East End. The air was heavy with fumes. With diesel particulates. Maybe ten years down the line, this walk might result in cancer. Unfair, as he was a pedestrian, an innocent party being showered in pollution.

The Gate Hotel was one of several small hotels on Romford Road in the Forest Gate area. Cheap, somewhat seedy. In the pre-motorcar days, Romford Road had been a droving trail for cattle and sheep, coming in from Essex into a hungry city. Still hungry, but now the animals were trucked in dead, motor traffic replacing herds and wagons.

He passed a Muslim girls' school, a crowd coming out, all chatter, in long black dresses and hijabs. It had formerly been a Methodist church, but Christians weren't so Christian these days, except for the African and Caribbean churches with happy clappy congregations packing fun into religion. Though the mosques held them without song and dance, busy with worshippers at sunset and kids going to after-school Koran classes.

The fear of God was still potent.

People who had left the area would say how much it had changed, and Jack didn't think they meant the architecture. But Jack had never felt threatened, though his mother did. More cut off than he was, isolated in her small church where loving your neighbour depended on your definition of love and of neighbour.

There was Katya on the other side of the road. She must be freezing in her short skirt and fishnet tights. She was talking to a black man, haggling probably. She couldn't go back to The Gate Hotel either. Had she another option?

He watched a little while, curious. She could go to another hotel. Do they book by the hour? That would put up her overheads, and the hotel could charge through the nose. She and the man were going off together, Katya taking short steps in her red high heels. Maybe she'd given him options, that was what the haggling was about. So much for a hotel, or ten quid discount for the back seat of his car.

At least she could work.

Jack turned into Woodgrange Road and headed for the Co-op. Might as well get some food for the next few days, with this enforced leisure. Though strolling around super-markets paid no bills. He'd laid out a lot of cash on this job, for materials and hiring a skip. Bob had loaned him the digger, some savings there, and he had insisted on Malik paying half upfront. Told him that he wouldn't start otherwise, having been bitten once too often by clients.

He was back home, putting his shopping away, when Alison rang. He knew she would. And more or less, what she would say when he'd said his piece.

'Mia says the cello hasn't come.'

'I can't get it there,' he said, waiting for the eruption.

'Why on earth not? You're only working a mile away. You could walk it there in twenty minutes.'

'My van is part of a crime scene.'

'A crime scene! Is someone dead in your van?'

'In the hotel I'm working at. They've made the hotel and car park a crime scene. I can't go to my van.'

'How do you do this, Jack?'

'I don't do anything. I was there working when a woman died. I didn't kill her, I don't know her from Eve. I didn't call the cops.'

'This wouldn't have happened if Mia had taken the cello into school.'

'She forgot. She left it in the van.'

'You forgot. You are her father.'

'Thank you for reminding me,' he said. 'I'd quite forgotten.'

'You know she has a concert? In less than a week. She has to practise. Her music teacher has phoned me twice.'

'I think you should get on to the police,' he said. 'Tell them to pack up their crime scene. Tell them Mia has a rehearsal. And if they don't do as you say, you'll get her music teacher on to them.'

'Very funny.'

'It amuses me.'

'You always were easily amused. Get the cello to my place. Your daughter must rehearse. I don't care how you do it, but do it. Nuff said. Bye, bye.'

She rang off.

He would if he could, that's what he would have said if there was anyone to say it to. She always left him with words in his mouth. A fight over a cello. It was ridiculous. She was ridiculous. Always ordering him about. But there was nothing he could do until the cops had gone.

Chapter 7

Fayyad told Geela to go out into the hall and remain there while he and Hayley interviewed her husband in the lounge. She was not pleased and demanded that she be present, but Fayyad was insistent. The alternative, he told her, was to take Malik to the station. She gave in and sat at the desk in the hall, arms folded, the constable at the door keeping his distance, but with half an eye to make sure she stayed in place.

Malik was seated in the middle of the sofa, his small frame reclining in the long seat. Fayyad and Hayley sat on wooden chairs facing him.

'You booked in the woman,' began Fayyad, 'let's call her Norma for want of her real name. You booked her into room 8.'

'I did. It's in the book, you've seen it.' He was almost sulky, like a teenager being admonished.

'But she ended up in room 6.'

'Her mistake. I don't know why. Except the key fits both doors.'

'We think there might be another explanation, Mr Bashir,' said Fayyad.

He shrugged as if he didn't care. 'I don't know what you mean.'

'We think you do, Mr Bashir,' exclaimed Hayley. 'You do realise that Norma will be given a vaginal swab?'

'I don't know what that is.'

'It's routine in rape cases,' she went on, 'but we will be asking for one in this. Her vaginal fluid will be tested.'

'So?' Malik shrugged.

'We think it's possible they'll find traces of your sperm,' said Fayyad.

Malik shuffled on the sofa. 'All nonsense. You're just trying to fit me up. I know your sort.'

Fayyad ignored the accusation, wondering if Malik might have shouted racism if Fayyad hadn't been Asian too.

'Let's make it plain,' he said. 'Did you have intercourse with Norma last night? Better if you tell us now, as we will certainly find out. And if it's shown that you lied to us, we will charge you with wasting police time.' Fayyad knew this was unlikely, too much hassle, but the threat often worked. 'So, let's have it. Did you have intercourse with the woman known as Norma Jean?'

Malik chewed his lower lip, he scratched his thighs.

'I want a solicitor,' he said.

'We're not accusing you of a crime, Mr Bashir. We are just trying to work out exactly what happened last night. We want to know why Norma was in room 6.'

'You won't tell my wife?'

'I can't make that promise, Mr Bashir. Although I've no intention of telling her as things stand, but I don't know where this investigation may lead.'

Malik raised his hands. 'All right, I slept with her. Please don't tell Geela.'

'So you wrote down room 8 in the register, but told her to go to room 6.'

'It's a better room.'

'It has a double bed,' said Hayley.

Malik gave a half grin.

'The screams in the night, they were from her?' said Fayyad.

'Sex games. She got very excited.'

'Did you hit her?'

'Only in play.'

'She has bruises on her side and back,' said Fayyad. 'Did you do those?'

'Of course not. I saw them. They were tender, I had to be careful.'

'They added to her screaming though.'

'She was excited. Very excited.'

'She was in pain,' said Hayley. 'Possibly drunk. Possibly rape, Mr Bashir.'

'Ridiculous. She agreed to sleep with me. Two adults. It happens all the time. This is a hotel. What do you think people use it for?'

'Let's get this clear,' said Fayyad. 'The woman came late last night. She wanted to book a room but had little money.'

'Just a few coins, not even a credit card.'

'So you did a deal with her. She could stay in exchange for sex.'

'It's not illegal,' said Malik morosely.

'It isn't. I just want to know what happened in that room. How long were you with her for?'

'I went to her room about ten past twelve. I stayed until about one.'

'How was she when you left?'

'Not dead, if that's what you mean. She was OK. Tired.'

'In pain?' enquired Hayley.

'A little. Not much. Sore I'd say.' He shuffled, stretched his legs.

'Was she drunk?'

'She was drinking,' he said. 'But the bottle wasn't empty when I left. Merry, I'd say. Excited.'

'One last point,' said Fayyad. 'If you knew she was in room 6 all the time, then why did you take the builder to the room?'

'I wanted an estimate for a job.'

'But Norma was in the room.'

'I thought she'd gone. I'd told her to leave before seven. That way Geela wouldn't ask why she hadn't paid. I didn't know she was still here. I told Fi she'd done a runner.'

'But she was in no condition to do any running.'

'How was I to know that? The last time I saw her, she was sleepy, a little drunk, but she'd be all right in a few hours. I'd told her to leave early, make the bed and take any rubbish with her. When I went up with Jack, I was caught out. I didn't know why the room was locked. I thought, she can't still be in there. It was past nine in the morning already. Then Fi came along. With the two of them there, I had no choice, we had to go in. I couldn't see what else to do. I thought if she was there, she'd be asleep. You know?'

'But she was dead,' said Hayley.

'I was as surprised as anyone. I thought she'd left.'

And not died in your hotel, thought Fayyad. Anywhere but here. Though he saw no point in voicing it. Sex, in his line of work, was often a brutal transaction.

'Thank you, Mr Bashir,' he said. 'I'm glad you've cleared up the matter for us.'

'Please don't tell Geela.'

PART TWO:
THE WOMAN IN ROOM 6

Chapter 8

Jack had phoned Malik who told him that the police had gone, along with the crime scene people. Without ado, Jack was quickly back at the hotel. He wanted to get the digging finished today if possible.

To one side of the driveway entrance were his materials: cubical sacks of sand and ballast, and smaller sacks of cement. The timber lay alongside with an encrusted cement mixer. It had obviously all come while he'd been away.

He went out the back and took his wheelbarrow out of his van. Seeing the cello, once again. He had to get it to the school. Soon, soon, do a little more here and then drop it over. Taking several trips, he wheelbarrowed the timber and cement from the front to the back parking area, where they'd be safer overnight.

Malik came out of the lounge.

'Those cops! Did they give me the third degree! Anyone would think I killed her.'

'Just doing their job,' said Jack.

'Am I glad they're gone. They want to know everything.'

'What's happening to the room?'

'I've let it for tonight.'

Jack screwed up his face.

'This is a hotel, mate. We let rooms. We've turned over the mattress. Clean sheets, clean duvet. A room's a room. We don't keep them empty if we can help it.'

'I wouldn't want to sleep in a bed someone's just died in.'

'We're not going to tell them. The room's clean, aired. Better than normal. It happens in hospitals all the time. Someone dies in a bed. Doesn't bother you if you don't know. Business is business. Anyway, before you deafen us with your digger, that job, I want an estimate.'

'Room 6. Forgot all about it with the fuss. You said you wanted it made into two rooms.'

'A sort of family suite. Can you do an estimate by tomorrow?'

'Let me get my tape. I'll take the measurements now.'

A few minutes later, they were in the room. The sash windows were wide open, the sound of the busy road pouring in, the smell of alcohol gone. The double bed was made up with a pale blue duvet over which floated white fluffy clouds. The pillows matched.

The room was devastatingly clean.

'So one room to become two rooms, with a connecting door,' said Malik.

'One window in each room?' said Jack.

'Yes.' Malik was striding about, imagining it. 'An internal door from room to room. And another in each to the corridor. So I can let them as a family suite or separate rooms.'

'They'd hear each other sneeze.'

Malik shrugged. 'What do you expect, cheap hotel? Wear earplugs if you're bothered. Here's the key. Do me an estimate. I'll be upstairs in the office.'

He left Jack.

The room was chilly with the windows wide open. About four hours ago a dead woman had been lying in the bed. She'd been tidied away, the mattress turned over, clean sheets. He could see her in the bed, duvet to her neck, face to one side. Dead. Peculiar word. Meaning what? No brain activity, blood ceasing to flow, rot setting in.

Jack shuddered. Morbid thoughts. In almost any room in an old house someone has died. That's the way it is. Most of us die in houses, many in bed. But not with Jack to witness it. He didn't believe in ghosts, but even so, he opened the door to the hallway.

He flipped the light switch, not so much to give light but to check. Not working. The light was dangling in the centre of the room in a circular, white paper shade. Above it was a ceiling rose, a twisted floral pattern, about 15 inches in diameter. That would be awkward as a new wall would cut it in two. So take out the rose. But what about the lighting in the two rooms?

Out of curiosity, he took the light bulb from one of the two standard lamps. Jack stood on a chair under the centre light, twisted out the bulb and put the other in. Surely it wouldn't be that simple?

He climbed off the chair and went to the switch by the door. He flipped it. It still didn't work. A loose connection somewhere, most likely. Not that it mattered to him. The ceiling rose would have to go as the new wall would go through it. Assuming there was nothing much wrong with the light, he could just make a spur and have a centre light in each room.

Jack put the bulb back in the standard lamp and set to measuring the room, doing a crude sketch in his notebook and putting lengths and heights on his diagram. He sat on the arm of the armchair and halted. This was where the woman's handbag had been, on the seat. Her clothes had been on the chair by the bed, shoes under it. An empty bottle of whisky on the floor. All cleaned away.

The room wasn't haunted, even if he felt uncomfortable. That was his fear of death. Besides, didn't you have to be murdered or die in some unnatural way to come back and wander the earth? Wanting justice or revenge.

Superstition.

It was odd, though, that she didn't have any luggage. There was a tale there, no doubt. All he knew was the ending.

Geela came in.

She was wearing a green shalwar kameez with a hijab. She was darker than her husband, her eyes deep set. Unlike Malik, she was slipping into middle aged plumpness.

She frowned as she looked around the room.

'What job has he got for you this time?'

Jack rose from the arm of the armchair. 'Mr Bashir wants an estimate for dividing this room in two.'

She grimaced. 'It'll be like two stables. They'll hear each other's television. This place!' She threw up her hands. 'It's squalor. You know that woman Katya?'

'I do.'

'One afternoon, I counted. Twelve men. In four hours.' Her hand went to her cheeks. 'How can men put their thing in that place? Filth. Every room it's going on.'

There must be some who stayed for other reasons, he thought. Sure, couples used cheap hotels for sex; he'd done it himself. And Katya for business.

'And drugs. I smell it, I've seen them, tottering down the hallway, big grin on their faces. I have to book them in. I know what they are going to do. Take lines of snow and go to it like barnyard animals.' She shook in fury. 'I hear it. See, I know the words. Snow, spice, O, hash, junk. The hallway is misty some nights. What am I doing in this place?'

She was appealing to him, but what could he say to her? That some men and women had dirty habits and came to places like this to indulge them. She knew that already. He couldn't find excuses for the human race.

'Animals,' she went on. 'I don't want to touch their hands when I take their money. I think, what is the credit card smeared with? And Malik wants you to make another two rabbit hutches! Well, I shall talk to him about that.' She walked about the room, looking at the walls and the windows. 'A woman died in that bed last night. And he's already got a booking for tonight. Tell me...' She came closer. 'Will making this room into two rooms add to the value of the property?'

Jack wasn't sure it would. Two small rooms. A family space. Malik must think it would bring more money in.

'It might,' he said, weighing it up. 'The plan is to put a dividing room in with a door in it. For a family.'

'A homeless family. The Council pays. Poor kids. Women trying to be respectable among prostitutes and drug addicts. Me too, trying, not so well. I'm so glad I can't have children. Not with him. Could I bring them up here?'

'But you don't live here.'

'We spend so much time here we might as well be.' She waved a disparaging hand. 'We have a house in Manor Park. But one of us always sleeps here overnight. To run the bar, to let in the late comers. It's existence, not a life. But why? When this property is worth millions.'

'You want to sell up?' he said, knowing the answer from her face.

'Tomorrow!' she exclaimed. 'Malik says another ten years. Ten years of this squalor? I wasn't brought up this way. My father is a lawyer in Birmingham. He came here once with my mother. They were shocked. I go to my parents on my own, never with Malik. My father says divorce him. Can you believe that? My father, a good Muslim man saying that. No one in my family is divorced. But if I do, Malik will have to sell. And why not? Don't I have the right? Malik couldn't have bought this hotel without my money. Money from my grandmother. So the place is as much mine as his. My father says if I divorce him I'll get half. Are you married yourself?'

'Divorced,' he said.

'How has it affected your wife?'

'She's a head teacher. She's fine.' He grinned. 'Glad to be rid of me.'

'I think you're all right. People divorce too easily in this country. You should have tried harder.' She waved her hands. 'Forget it. I'm being a busybody.' She came in close. 'Tell me something. Don't hide it. Is Malik sleeping with Fi?'

'No,' he said, surprised at the question.

'I've seen her touch him. She's cheeky to him. Not like a worker should be with her boss.'

'It's just joshing,' he said. 'She's not sleeping with Malik.' It had never occurred to him. Malik had got him the theatre ticket with her. He wasn't her type.

'I think he'd like to get rid of me and marry her.'

'I'm sure that's not true,' said Jack.

It was likely Malik had the hots for Fi, and that's what Geela was picking up on. But he couldn't believe Fi would go for Malik. He was married, but that didn't rule out an affair. Jack just couldn't imagine her fancying him.

'Are you going to marry again?' she said.

'Who knows?' he said. 'I have to meet someone first. Someone I want, someone who wants me. I'm not the easiest person to get along with.'

'Me neither,' she said. She smiled. 'I like talking to you. Do you know this would be considered disgraceful in my religion? Talking to a man without my husband present. That's what I was taught. But twelve years in this place and I have lost my standards. You see what's happening? How will I end up?'

'This place isn't right for you,' he said. His too-obvious advice for a middle-aged Muslim woman.

'Thank you for listening to me,' she said. 'I know you have work to do, other than listen to my silly moans.'

'They're not silly,' he said. 'I couldn't stick this place. But then I don't have to. I'll be gone in a few days. But you...'

'I'll still be here. Year in, year out. Unless I take steps.' She sighed. 'I haven't got a fairy godmother.' She went to the door. 'Thank you. You have helped me think things through.'

Chapter 9

Jack locked room 6 and went up the stairs to the hotel office. He'd not been up to the top floor before. The ceiling was low, only a foot or so above his head. It was evident that it had been the loft space but had been converted into five rooms. Stables, thought Jack. There were three numbered rooms, another labelled 'Bathroom' and the other 'Office'.

Jack knocked on the office door.

'Who is it?' called Malik.

'Jack, with the key.'

'Come in.'

Jack entered. The office was small with a sloping ceiling, a window set into it, stained with bird droppings. The space was muggy and quite packed out: two filing cabinets, a set of shelves loaded with papers and folders, with barely room for the desk which Malik sat behind. At one side of it was a folded camp bed, held in place by a column of sheets, duvet and pillows.

Malik closed a large red ledger as Jack entered. 'Almost caught me in the act.'

'I'd have thought you'd have your accounts computerised,' said Jack.

'Ask me no questions about bookkeeping,' said Malik with a wink. 'I'm sure you can be quite creative yourself. Take a seat, I'd like a word.' He rose and took the papers off the only other chair, and Jack sat down. 'My wife's been talking to you.'

'How do you know?'

'I heard her yapping when I was coming up here. What's she been saying? Nothing nice, I'm sure.'

'She doesn't like The Gate Hotel,' said Jack, considering what to say to her husband, and deciding only to tell him what he already knew. 'Thinks it's a bad place for a Muslim woman.'

'That's her family talking. Bunch of Birmingham snobs. Give me ten years, I'll be worth ten times the lot of them. What else?'

'She wants to sell up.'

'She tells me that every day, Jack.' He laughed, slapping the desk. 'Did she tell you that I was sleeping with Fi?'

'No.'

'She tells me I am. I wish, I wish. But let me inform you, I am not. Don't get me wrong, I wouldn't kick Fi out of bed. But she's not having any. Geela wants to sack her. I say – a good worker like her, never. Comes in at six in the morning, works like a slave for four hours. Where would we get someone like her?'

'Sounds like one big happy family.'

'I'm happy when I come to the hotel,' said Malik. 'And Geela's at home. I can breathe. Even when we are both here it's OK, with all the people to keep us apart. She's at the desk down the bottom, I'm up here in the rooftop. Three floors between us, not gabbing at me like at home. Sell up! Sell up! Leave those low-lives to wallow in their own filth. She doesn't understand. Here people listen to me. I'm in charge. OK, some are not so respectable. But everyone has to live their life. Who am I to judge?'

'It's not the place for a good Muslim.'

'Whoever said I was a good Muslim? They're lying!' He laughed. 'No one will charge me with that. But I don't drink alcohol. OK, I sell the stuff to Kafirs, let rooms to Kafir junkies and couples who want a space no-questions-asked. I'm like a Muslim trader on the Silk Road, making the best of conditions where I find them. I'm not here to change morals. I'm not a prophet. The locals will carry on their dirty habits with or without me.'

Jack smiled at Malik's philosophy. Just making a living, as Jack was himself. Here under the roof, his home from home, the filing cabinets, the bed, the dodgy accounts, atop his besmirched kingdom. Looking about, he spotted two large hooks just below the window.

'What are the hooks for?'

'A fire precaution,' said Malik. 'I've a rope ladder.' He lifted it from behind his desk, expanding the rungs like a concertina. 'If she ever decides to put a fire under me, I'll attach it to those hooks and get down to the fire escape. I've tried it once. Quite exhilarating if you've a head for heights. I was like Spiderman.'

'I hope you never have to use it for real.'

'Me too. That would be disaster. I bet she's considered it. Though the hotel is insured. That's a disaster too. The price of it. And it goes up and up.' He smiled. 'You see how I live. I talk to everyone. I'm not a judge with a wig and gown, like my wife. That's why she's so unhappy. But I tell you, Jack, you can't change human nature. Adjust to it, tune in, like the hippies used to say.'

'Turn on,' added Jack.

'Coffee and tea, I limit myself to. Conversation is my drug.'

'Cheap,' said Jack rising. 'Here's the key to room 6.' He placed it on the desk. 'I must get back to work. I'd like to finish the digging before I leave tonight.'

'And then go to the theatre with our lovely soap star,' said Malik with a smirk. 'Don't keep her up too late, my good fellow.'

Chapter 10

Fayyad was in the office of his chief, Detective Superintendent Nikki Martin. He was sitting opposite her wide desk. The space was roomy, promotion equalling expanse, with its book filled shelving, coffee table, even an armchair, which she rarely used, offering it to guests. Sinking deep in its cushions, they gave her the height advantage.

DS Martin was a stocky, middle aged woman who'd come up through the ranks. She wore a dress suit, the jacket over the back of her swivel chair, no make up. Her blonde hair was short and practical. No need for tedious brushing.

'So most likely, a heart attack of an unknown, penniless woman,' she said. 'The hotel owner admits to sleeping with her in exchange for a room, dubious but no crime.' She sat back in her high backed chair. 'I think we've come to the end of this one, Fayyad. I can't justify keeping you on it. We'll get some posters made up, put them around here and there. 'Do you know this woman?' sort of thing. Notify the press. And see what happens with the autopsy. My betting is they'll not come up with anything other than natural causes. The manager leaves her, the woman locks herself in, probably to stop him coming back. And in the morning she's dead. It happens.'

Fayyad couldn't argue with her analysis, but something was niggling at him.

'It's no ID that bothers me,' he said. 'No credit card, not a letter. It doesn't feel right.'

'You think she was murdered?'

'I'm not saying that.'

'Anything else is not our concern, Fayyad.'

'She was a battered woman.'

He was interrupted by Hayley putting her head round the door.

'Excuse me butting in, ma'am. But I've some evidence you might like to see.'

'Come in and sit down, Hayley. Show us what you've got.'

Hayley took the other wooden chair and placed a transparent plastic evidence-bag on the desk. There was a fragment of a train ticket in it.

'The crime scene people found it in the woman's shoe. Didn't spot it at first, it was down in the toe,' said Hayley.

DS Martin twisted the bag round. 'It says 'She'. Could that be Sheffield? The woman might be a northerner.'

'It has a time on it, ma'am. See here, tiny writing.' Hayley pointed it out. 'It says: Printed 22.28'. The date is ripped off. But I think it could have been last night.'

'The woman signed in at the hotel at 11.20 pm,' said Fayyad.

'If so, it can't be Sheffield,' said his boss. 'She couldn't travel 200 miles in 50 minutes.'

'I think it's Shenfield, ma'am,' said Hayley.

'Of course!' DS Martin slapped her hands together. 'What was I thinking? Of course, Shenfield. It's on the line from Forest Gate.'

'A 30 minute journey,' said Hayley. 'I've checked it out. She could have caught the 22.36 last night and been in Forest Gate at 11.06 pm.'

'It's less than a ten minute walk from the station to The Gate Hotel,' said Fayyad.

'It certainly fits,' admitted DS Martin. 'But this could be an old ticket. No date on it. But it's the best we have, so worth a follow up.'

'I've already phoned Shenfield station,' said Hayley. 'They've got CCTV covering anyone coming in to the station. I thought I could go there. With your permission, ma'am. Catch the train, just 30 minutes from Forest Gate. And look through the footage.'

'Do so,' said her boss. 'Right away. No, first get a poster made up. Leave it at the station if you find her on the footage. Well done, Hayley. Good initiative. Off you go and savour the delights of Shenfield.'

'I'd rather go to Sheffield.'

DS Martin laughed. 'The budget won't stretch. It's a night out in Shenfield, I'm afraid.'

Chapter 11

Jack had finished the digging and levelling of the ground. It was close to five thirty; it had been dark for over an hour and he'd had to work by the light of the hotel. As the sun had lowered the temperature had fallen, and it was close to freezing when he stopped work, his feet and fingers painful. He'd need to check the ground again in the morning as it was likely the cold had dulled him and made him careless in his levelling. But enough for today. He must warm up, get some energy for his theatre date. Half of him wanted to go home and stay there in warmth. Stretch out in front of the TV. The other half knew he'd regret not going out with Fi. If he didn't turn up, that would be the beginning and end of any relationship.

He removed the ignition key from Betelgeuse and packed his wheelbarrow in his van.

The cello!

There, accusing him. Alison had said something about Mia's concert, her irate music teacher. Well, he was cold, too cold. Let tomorrow take care of it.

He drove home.

There, he showered and shaved. The heat was wonderful. Soaking through to his bones, putting life back. At least tomorrow he wouldn't be sitting on the digger all day and could stay warm by working. His bathroom was like a steam bath; he'd stayed under the shower so long his fingers had ripples. He rubbed himself down with the towel. Pity it wasn't a clean one, it would have been so nice to have a soft, fresh towel. But you can't have everything. He put on clean clothes though, a date after all: jeans, a polo top and a jumper that Alison had bought for him when they were together. He must get some more clothes; he had a tendency to wear them when painting or plastering, and ruining them. That's what overalls are for: to protect clothing.

Enough lectures.

He calculated it would take an hour to the pub theatre. And he'd need to eat first as this was a post dinner date. Pleased with himself for shopping when he had the enforced leisure time earlier today, he had a toasted cheese and bacon sandwich. That would last him. Though they could get something after the show, but that might be ten o'clock or later. He was nervous. Theatre wasn't his thing. He'd never been out with an actress before. He hoped his ignorance wouldn't be exposed.

He mustn't run ahead of himself, thinking what might happen after. Don't rush headlong. He knew nothing about her; she might have a boyfriend who happened to be out of town tonight. Above all, don't look desperate.

Might she like a night out with the telescope? That was his thing, rather than a play. She just might. And then marry him and settle down with him in the country when her rich aunt died and left her a manor house. And so forth.

Ready to go, he put on his blue, padded winter jacket, a scarf and a woolly hat, a last look in the mirror, his hair was thinning at the front. He'd overdone the aftershave. He went back in the bathroom and wiped his cheeks on the damp towel. That must be better as the towel smelt of aftershave.

He left the house. There was a chilly breeze but he was dressed for cold. He knew from years of working outside to not skimp on clothing on winter days. You can take off a layer but you can't put on what you haven't brought with you. He walked past his van, giving it a pat, as if it were a faithful horse. Jack wasn't going to drive there. It was easy enough to get to the Angel by public transport, with plenty of options for getting home.

The trees on both sides of Earlham Grove were black in the streetlights, revealing, in their bleakness, the cutting back they suffered year after year, in the thick knuckling at the ends of the main branches. Winter anguish. Which he knew was nonsense, they were plants. But he was out on a date, with a head full of hope and fancy.

Jack turned onto the high street, busy with traffic and the footfall of the rush hour. He was going in to the city, so he'd avoid the crush which was mostly the other way, the commuters going home to the outer London boroughs and Essex. He should've brought his astronomy magazine for the journey. Too bad. There was usually a free paper lying around.

At the station, Jack bought his ticket at the ticket office, and coming out of the ticket office almost bumped into Hayley as she turned away from the ticket machine. She had a cardboard tube under her arm like Charlie Chaplin's walking stick.

'You're looking smart, Jack. I smell aftershave. Where you off to?'

'Up Islington,' he said. 'The theatre.'

'With someone nice?' she said slyly.

'I hope so. Where you going?'

'Still working,' she said. 'I'm off to Shenfield. It's possible that dead woman is from there.'

'Norma Jean,' he said. 'Strange that she had no ID.'

'We found half a ticket that we think is from Shenfield. Someone must be missing her. So I'll see if we can track her down. I've got to look through CCTV footage. And if I spot her, leave a poster.' She tapped the cardboard tube under her arm.

The Shenfield train was announced.

'Must run,' she said. 'Hope your date goes well.'

And she was swiftly off.

The Shenfield train was on the other line, going the opposite way to his. Down on the platform, he watched her train come in, crowded with commuters going home. He couldn't see her get on, she'd probably have to stand, but would likely get a seat at Ilford, only a couple of stations down the line, where many people alighted.

He reflected on what Hayley had told him about Norma Jean. She might have come from Shenfield, the last stop on Hayley's train. She would have arrived late last night at the hotel, no luggage, and no ID. Norma Jean was likely running from someone.

And ended up dead in a hotel room in Forest Gate.

Five minutes later, his train arrived. Jack took a seat facing forward, on the right. Beyond Stratford, he liked to see the Olympic Park. Especially at night, in the lights. The train would pass the swimming pool, designed by some famous architect, that Iranian woman, and then the stadium which was now home to West Ham. He'd gone there a few weeks back to watch a match. The tickets were pricey, how anyone afforded a season ticket these days... The pitch was further back than at the Upton Park ground, because of the running track, but not as bad as people said it would be.

West Ham had lost. Which always felt a waste of money, as you went home feeling lousy.

Half the train emptied at Stratford with its motley inter-changes. He wondered how Fi would be outside the hotel. He'd only seen her in work clothes, spoken to her in the kitchen for ten minutes when she'd given him breakfast. Not quite a blind date, but close to. She might surprise him by telling him she was getting married in a month. Or going off to New York to play on Broadway. Assume nothing, he told himself for the twelfth time. It's a visit to the theatre, enjoy it, and whatever happens after that happens. Or doesn't happen. Though it was impossible not to anticipate, and hope.

The train was passing the lit up Olympic pool when Alison phoned. The instant he saw her name on the screen, he knew what this was about. All his daydreaming about Fi slapped down to earth.

'Where's the cello?'

He knew exactly where it was, had even seen when he put the wheelbarrow away, but showering, changing, eating, and what he'd say and wouldn't say had pushed the instrument aside. Although he knew that if he hadn't been so cold and numb, he could've dropped it over after work.

'In the van.'

'Bring it over now.'

'I'm on the train,' he said. 'I won't be back till late.'

'Not in a crime scene any more?'

'I forgot. Sorry.'

'Your daughter's concert is in a couple of days, Jack. It may not be important to you, but do you want her to be the one out of tune in the orchestra?'

What on earth could he say to that? Of course he didn't. He should have dropped it off after work. He should have written it down, tied a string on his finger, put Post-It notes about his body. Sex made him forget things, took priority.

'I'll bring it over first thing.'

She rang off. In disbelief, he guessed. He'd better be there with the cello in the morning. Apologise to Fi. No, she'd already be gone, starting work at six. He felt in his pockets for a pen. Nowhere, and nothing to write on either. He tried to think of some way to remember. Cello, yellow, ring the bello for the fellow, who is going to get hell-o if he continues to forget the mellow cello.

Chapter 12

It was warmer and misty as Jack went down Upper Street towards the pub. Lights from shops and street lamps glowed through the fog. His breath showed in front of him. He had been walking quickly once he'd left the Angel tube, but had now slowed up. He didn't know what to expect; would she introduce him to her friends and they ask him about the play? What would he say? In a pub, of all places. After more than two years on the wagon, pubs were the whores of Babylon, the temptress, the come hither smiles, the beckoning lips proffering the brimming liquid, so jolly, so easy to join in the fun. And end up with a gashed head and a gut full of vomit, wondering how he got where he was.

Alcohol Halt, in one of its many mantras, said: stay out of places where you might be snared.

Too late for that. He'd arrived at the King's Head, a Victorian pub with a floral pattern on the frosted window. It wasn't really his sort of place, not even in his drinking days. A pub in Islington, full of intellectuals talking about art galleries and the opera. He walked past it and onwards, down the road, away. He'd gather courage in a few minutes, turn back and burst in. By that time Fi would be there already, so he wouldn't have to wait alone with strangers all drinking brown liquids.

Jack passed animated restaurants, smokers outside another pub, a man with a brazier selling hot chestnuts, individuals and couples looming out of the mist. He'd walk to the traffic lights and turn round.

Theatre. To be or not to be... The last time he'd gone was when he and Alison had taken Mia to the Theatre Royal in

Stratford. *Jack and the Beanstalk*, the principal boy was a girl, the dame was a TV comic whose name he couldn't remember...

'Jack!'

She was coming towards him. He never would have recognised her. She was wearing a bright red coat and a white woolly hat with red reindeer running round it and a red bobble. She took his arm and reversed his direction.

'I must have missed it,' he said. 'I was day dreaming.'

'About what?'

'About the woman I was about to meet and the wonderful play I was going to see.'

He felt her arm in his, the easy lightness. What was there to be afraid of?

'Have I got to sweep you off your feet?' she said.

'We'll dance all night,' he said.

'And I'll go into work at six and weep into the frying bacon.'

'Why will you weep?'

There might have been no one else. The shops and traffic had disappeared, the passers-by were bit players without lines, dismissed once he and she had gone by. The mist had been ordered, the streetlights going off one by one, as they passed.

'Because I'm alone in the kitchen,' she said. 'And I have another day to get through.' She stopped. 'Enough of this, I don't want to think about work. It's a night out. Let's not go straight in, let's walk a while. I want to talk to you. We'll go back at five to eight, then we can go straight into the theatre and we won't have to buy a drink. In fact, I don't like to drink before a play as I'm usually bursting by the interval.'

'I'm happy to be walking,' he said.

They'd come to the King's Head. Two men outside were smoking, one of them said something about Arsenal, West Ham's London rivals. Not opera or art galleries.

She said, 'Do you believe in ghosts?'

He turned to her. Her lipstick matched the red of her coat and of the reindeer and bobble.

'Strange question.'

'I'll tell you why in a minute. Just answer me.'

Another bossy woman. He seemed to be attracted to them. Women who could direct him and change his life. Until he found he didn't want what they wanted of him. Dooming this one before their relationship had begun. Give her a chance!

'I don't think I believe in ghosts,' he said. 'Though I wouldn't want to walk through a graveyard at midnight.'

'I believe in them,' she said. 'I've seen one. I can sense the atmosphere, I can feel the presence.'

'When did you see one?'

'The first time was five years ago. I was staying at a National Trust cottage in Suffolk with my then boyfriend, Al. It was two in the morning and we'd had a row. That's another story. I won't go into it.' She flapped a hand in dismissal. 'Usual stuff. Anyway, I couldn't sleep, so I went down the stairs in my dressing gown and slippers, to go to the kitchen to munch something. And saw, sitting on the bottom step, a girl, about ten. She had a long dress on, down to her ankles and a big floppy hat so I could hardly make out her face. She said, 'Have you seen Maria?' I couldn't answer, I was so surprised to see her. I touched her to find out if she was real. And she screamed and kept screaming. I could see into the black of her throat, like a great cave. I ran upstairs, and woke up Al in my panic. He came down with me and there was no one there. He thought I was delusional. He was a mathematician. Very rational. We had a final row.'

'I can see why,' he said. Though he was not sure that he could, but best be on the side of the one you are with.

'I can sense ghosts. Feel them. They walk the earth when something dreadful has happened. Like in Hamlet.'

He knew Hamlet was a Shakespeare play. He didn't know anything about a ghost in it.

'I'm trying to think about the ghost in Hamlet...' he tried, hoping she'd help out.

'You know,' she said, as if everyone did. 'It's his father's ghost. He comes on the battlements of Elsinore castle night after night, to give Hamlet a message. That he was murdered by his brother, Hamlet's uncle, who has now married Gertrude, Hamlet's mother.'

'Very incestuous,' said Jack, trying to keep up with the family relationships.

'The ghost has to be appeased,' she said. 'That's Hamlet's problem. He's just a student. And now he has to revenge his father.' She stopped. 'Enough about Hamlet. Let's head back to the theatre.' They turned about and began walking back the way they had come.

'Why are you asking me about ghosts?' he said.

'It's room 6,' she said. 'The one where we found the woman.'

'How can I forget it? It was only this morning.'

'It's haunted,' she said. 'You remember I went all dizzy...'

'I do. You'd felt the woman's face and neck. And found she was dead.'

'It wasn't that she was dead. I was sorry but not knocked out about her. I didn't know her. But I'd felt a ghost. A presence. Someone was stalking the room. Do you believe me?'

'Of course I do.' In the room when he was measuring up, he'd had thoughts of ghosts. But only thoughts. So of course he believed her, walking arm in arm.

'A woman it was. From about a hundred years ago. I think she was murdered there.'

That surprised him. 'Not the ghost of Norma Jean?'

'No. Too soon for her. She won't come back, if she comes back, for ten years or more. I felt another woman, much earlier...'

'Have you felt her before?'

'I have. From the first time I went into the room; I thought, there's a presence here. Now, I only go in there in daylight. If the curtains are shut, I close my eyes, go in and instantly rip them wide open. I keep the door open too. I do the room as fast as I can. I sing. Don't laugh.'

'I'm not laughing. But what has the ghost to do with Norma Jean's death?'

They'd arrived back at the King's Head.

'I think she died of fright,' said Fi.

Chapter 13

Hayley was on the office computer. Not the best place to work, as she could hear all the station announcements for the trains going in and out of Shenfield. Some were recorded and came from the machine in this office, others from the woman seated nearby, made directly into her microphone. After an hour of it, Hayley could have made them herself, having heard repeatedly about trains on their way to Southend, to Liverpool Street, to Chelmsford, going out to Colchester, Ipswich, and Norwich. All announced loudly, clearly and too often for her.

Irritating, but she'd got to the point of almost shutting them out. The footage she was watching was silent, taken from the CCTV camera which was directed at those coming in through the barrier to go on to the platforms. She'd noted two teenagers jumping the barrier, a minor crime, someone else's job.

She made no conversation with the station woman who between announcements was busy with paperwork. Hayley was impressed by her efficiency, but then again, it was routine, the same trains coming and going, unless there were delays and apologies. Which of course there were. Beginning with the tail end of rush hour, incredibly busy as the commuters came home from their day's work in London. Quieter, once that was over, with people going back into town for work or leisure.

Hayley wanted to be at home with her wife, Alice. She'd had too many late nights recently. But she'd set herself up for this job, guessing where the ticket was from and checking they had CCTV. Being in DS Martin's good books mattered to her. She'd go up a peg too, if she found the woman. Though it would make more work. A trip to Norma's home, one of those awful visitations, when you never know how you'll be received. Earlier in her career, she'd worked in the traffic police. She always remembered a mother's distress when she had to tell her that her six year old son had been run over by a car. There is no way of saying such things without transmitting pain, any sympathy useless.

Thinking ahead, she wondered about this home visit. If Norma was from around here. If Hayley could find her. Norma was bruised, which suggested domestic violence. A male partner most likely. A woman could not be ruled out, though statistically less likely. Men were stronger, lesbian couples more equally matched. In general, always the proviso; a detective must not forget there are always exceptions.

Hayley had wanted to be a detective from her first day in the force, six years ago. She'd taken the exams and passed well. Step one. She liked working with Fayyad. He wasn't macho like some other officers she could name, nor prone to inane remarks like 'how's the weather up there?' Or allusions to lesbian sex as if it were still regarded as weird.

Early on, she had realised that if she was going to work in what was still a male stronghold, then she mustn't bridle at every slight. Most could be shrugged off. With the more pointed, she was learning the art of the humorous comeback, like a comedian dealing with hecklers.

Hit hard, but be funny.

The CCTV footage was conveniently dated and timed, which meant she could concentrate on the relevant time of day. The ticket was timed 22.28. She'd asked the station woman how accurate the ticket machine was. Spot on, she'd been told, but the CCTV was a couple of minutes out. So Hayley had begun at 22.10 and was going through the footage, stopping if she had any doubt. On her phone were several photos so that she could check the woman's face, coat, handbag and shoes.

That time of night, yesterday, the station had been quiet, just a few people every minute, so they could be mostly seen clearly. In the rush hour, identification would have been difficult with the flood of people going through. Here it was single men and women, and some couples; not likely for her woman, but she mustn't rule it out. She had no interest in those leaving the station. They were just backs on this footage. Another camera caught their faces, irrelevant to her. Norma Jean, if she had come into Shenfield station, would be going in, in order to catch a train to Forest Gate.

Why Forest Gate, Hayley thought. Could be random, she had to get off somewhere, even if she was just running away. Could have been anywhere along the line. Or maybe she knew someone in Forest Gate. Too big an area to go door to door with photos, but a poster at the station might result in an identification.

On the footage, a couple was coming to the barrier. Behind them a woman Hayley couldn't see too well. The woman was too close to the couple, walking rapidly, almost hidden by them. Hayley stopped the footage and played it again, slow – frame by frame. That was the handbag. That could well be the coat, but the light altered its colour. She went for a still and zoomed in on the woman's face. It was her! The nose, the hair. Poor woman, running from something perhaps, into something worse.

She captured the relevant pictures on a memory stick, and before leaving Shenfield, stuck a poster on a board at the entrance. She had another with her. This one, she'd put up at Forest Gate. There could well be a reason why Norma had alighted there.

Chapter 14

It was the worst play Jack had ever seen. Not that there were that many on his list, if you don't count cop shows on TV or Doctor Who. A few pantomimes could be counted and one play from school. His English teacher had taken the class to see Macbeth. She had told them about the play beforehand: about the witches, Macbeth's ambition and his wife's part in it. Jack had expected to be bored silly, but to his surprise he'd quite enjoyed it. The language was tough going, but he knew it was rich. There was a ghost in it, Banquo's. Fancy remembering that. Weird name. Lots of killing, maybe that's what had appealed to his teenage appetite. Macbeth had started off as a good guy and ended up a murdering dictator. And there was some ace sword fighting near the end. 'Lay on, Macduff!' He recollected that line where Macbeth and Macduff slashed at each other with their swords, to the very end. Which was Macbeth's head dangling from Macduff's fist. Clever how they made that look real.

He liked action; this play had none. It was all talk.

There were about twenty in the audience. Fi had insisted on sitting in the front row, wooden chairs, presumably you would forget the hardness if you were enthralled. But boredom made his chair as hard as marble. After half an hour, he took off his jacket and folded it under him as a cushion. There were three actors, sitting on chairs too, looking out at the audience, never at each other. Two men and a woman, the woman being Fi's friend. Every so often the lights would go out and when they came back on again, the actors had switched places. Jack didn't find that at all exciting, not compared with a sword fight. But beyond that, he didn't know what they were talking about. Were they dead? Almost dead, in hell?

Did he care?

An hour can be a long time on a wooden chair. The most interesting bit was when Fi held his hand. He wondered what she was trying to say. This is a good bit, a bad bit. Or simply, I'm still alive. Are you?

He let his mind wander, considering what Fi had told him as they'd walked. She genuinely believed Norma Jean had died of fright. He could accept you could die of boredom, but of fright? If something was so terrifying, then your heart rate would race to its maximum – and then fail, maybe. It sounded possible. Google it later. It presupposed the woman had seen something to be afraid of. A ghost, Fi had said, of a woman who had been murdered in room 6 a hundred years before.

The three on chairs were still talking. He listened again for a few minutes. It still didn't make sense.

A ghost had killed Norma, according to Fi. He imagined it as a defence in court:

It wasn't me, your honour. It was a ghost. I just happened to be there at the time, and was so scared I couldn't do a thing to help. My first witness is a medium.

Fi wouldn't appreciate his take on it. He'd keep his humour to himself. Norma Jean was dead. That could be agreed on. Maybe heart attack. But a ghost as the cause?

Far fetched.

But Fi believed such stuff. He didn't. If he took the mickey, she'd get angry. It would never last. Was it worth starting? Get it in proportion, there weren't ghosts all the time. Agree to disagree. He returned to the play. It made as little sense as before, the three actors had tried all permutations of three in a line. Six, Jack worked out. And he checked it, having plenty of time to do so. If they'd done them all, it must mean the first act was coming to an end.

Please.

It did end. The lights suddenly went out. And when they came on again, the chairs were empty. Jack almost cheered. The interval. Freedom! What was he supposed to say to Fi? Maybe she loved it, the poetry, the symbolism, her friend's magnificent acting. It would never work out.

'What do you think?' she said.

He was stuck. He couldn't say he thought it terrible. Maybe it wasn't. It could be him, his knowledge of plays. Or rather, lack of. Fi's friend was in it. She was waiting for his response. Something had to be said.

'It's difficult,' he managed to say. 'I got lost.'

'Me too, Jack,' she said. 'You don't have to pretend. It was awful. I can't believe how awful it was.'

Jack sighed with relief.

'I thought I was going to have to lie to you,' he said. 'I've never been so bored in my life.'

'Let's go and stretch our legs.'

They went out of the theatre and through the bar, which was busy with the added theatre crowd. Hardly crowd. Family and friends most likely. They went outside the pub, where there were others, mostly smoking. The mist had grown thicker, beams from cars and buses painted the droplets yellow. The weather was changing. Might there be a clear night tomorrow?

'What a terrible set,' she said. 'Three people on chairs. Nothing else. Where's the imagination? I started off as a stage manager, you know, before I got my first acting job. I could have come up with something much better. I was a half decent carpenter. See me with a drill and a circular saw. Not that a better set would have improved the play. Still be a dirge.' She stopped and chewed her bottom lip. 'What do you think it was about?'

'Life and death?' he hazarded, on the grounds that most things were, especially when you couldn't understand them.

She nodded. 'I expect so. Always a safe reply. I'm going to have to say something to Sarah.'

Jack twisted his neck and rubbed his backside. 'Oh, those seats are hard. Do we have to go back?'

'You leave if you want to, Jack. Sorry it's so bad. I hate it when it's like this. Lousy play, which I inflict on someone else, and then because my friend's in it, I have to stay to the very end. And clap.'

'I'll stay,' he said.

'You don't have to. Please don't feel any obligation.'

'I'll let my mind wander,' he said. 'In the first half, I was thinking about your ghost.'

'The one that killed Norma Jean?'

'Yes, the lady who was murdered 100 years ago.'

'Do you believe in her?'

'No.' He might not have said that if he'd enjoyed the play. Simply gone along with Fi. But he hadn't enjoyed it and was going to stick it out for her sake, so he was allowed to be honest. See how she reacted. If they had a chance to move on.

'I'm psychic,' she said. 'There's a ghost in that room, believe me.'

'I don't know what to say,' he said.

'Come and look at the room with me tomorrow.'

He agreed, as much to close the subject as his curiosity. To get off the subject, he asked her about her rehearsal today. She said it was a good escape from the events at the hotel but she'd had to apologise to everyone for being late. Or rather being later than usual, as she was always late but the others knew that her job meant she couldn't get away till ten. And allowed for it. At least a dead woman gave her an excuse for being later than usual. It was a good play, but she was behind on learning her lines. Some of them were off the book, while she'd barely begun. No money in it but she was happy to be working amongst professionals. It made her feel like an actor instead of a cook.

The chill had penetrated, so they went back inside. A few minutes later, the bell rang for the second act.

Chapter 15

It was worse than the first act. This time round Jack knew there would be no surprises. Just three people on chairs who switched at each blackout, and would carry on switching for the full six possible permutations. And then it would end.

Finite at least.

He thought about the cello, which he had to get back on pain of Alison. Or his daughter would be shown up at her concert, which he should go to. Thursday. He should have a pen with him. Normally he did, but he'd changed his clothes. He thought about the ghost which he didn't believe in, and what on earth would Fi show him when they looked at the room tomorrow? Maybe she had one of those machines to catch ghostly wails.

He thought about how ghastly the play was. Of all his scenarios with Fi this afternoon, he hadn't anticipated a lousy play that he would sit through to the end. At least she thought it bad too. So perhaps there was a chance. And she wasn't upset he was sceptical about ghosts. Though she might try to convert him tomorrow. Like one of those bible bashers who came to the front door. With all the answers and leaflets.

Eight others endured the second act. Probably all friends of the cast. He couldn't believe a single one of them was enjoying it. It wasn't possible. How had the play been put on? Did no one in the cast realise it was rubbish?

How does it happen, those plays that close after two days? The actors, the backers, the director, must have believed in it at one point. How does it get past them all? These three actors, how had they convinced themselves?

Did they know really and were hiding it, or did they believe this was a work of genius?

Perhaps it was. Too deep for him. Maybe it was all poetry and philosophy, way over his head. Why wouldn't they look at each other? Why did each one pretend they were the only one on the stage? Perhaps that was the answer. We are all alone, we spend our lives talking to ourselves.

Perhaps.

At long last the lights went down, and came up on three empty chairs. Eight people applauded as the cast came out holding hands and bowing. Someone shouted 'bravo'. Jack clapped furiously, pleased it was done with and they could escape.

But not quite. Fi said that they should go backstage. That's what you did. It was expected, she said. She led him by the hand through a side curtain, to the dressing room. It was a room with a central light bulb but most of the light came from lights around the mirrors over sinks. The three cast members were each seated in front of one, wiping off make-up. The room was hot and pungent with grease paint.

Fi went at once to Sarah and clasped her in her arms.

'You were wonderful, darling.'

Jack couldn't believe people actually said that. He thought that it was just on TV. That no one actually said it.

Maybe they learnt it off TV.

Sarah said, as she wiped the make-up from her face, 'Quite a few of the audience didn't come back after the interval.'

'It's quite intellectual,' said Fi carefully. 'It does test you. And not everyone wants to think about life and death. They want escapism.'

Sarah smiled. Fi had hit the right note.

'We're going to make a few cuts before the critics come in two days. Any thoughts where?'

First and second act, thought Jack.

'I don't know specifically where,' said Fi. 'I'd have to read the text. But maybe it's a line by line thing. Make it tighter.'

'Thank you so much for coming, darling.'

They embraced again.

'I'm in a lunchtime piece at the Lamb and Flag in a week,' said Fi.

'Oh, I must come.'

Jack hadn't said a word, relieved the two women were chatting. But then Sarah turned to him.

'And what did you think of it, Malik?'

Fi instantly corrected her. 'This isn't Malik. He had a family crisis, so Jack said he'd come.'

Jack didn't quite remember it like that. Malik had pushed him into it.

'Oh, you and your men, Fi. I can't keep up with you.'

That struck Jack. Fi had a trail of admirers? She collected them, it seemed. And he was one, having stayed to watch the most mind numbing piece in the universe. He wouldn't have done it for just anyone, though. He was suddenly aware Sarah was staring at him. She must have said something.

'Can you repeat that?' he had to say.

'Did you like it?' she said, with a wonderful smile, inviting only one answer.

'Very dramatic,' he managed to say, knowing it was stupid as soon as it came out. There wasn't a dramatic moment in it. 'I mean, your concentration. How you totally ignored each other. Isolated in your own bubble. Alone in the world.'

'Quite intelligent, this one,' said Sarah with a smirk at Fi.

'Stop it,' exclaimed Fi, punching her on the shoulder. She turned to Jack, gave a nod, then back to Sarah. 'We really must go.'

More embraces followed. First Fi kissed Sarah on either cheek. Then the two men, telling them too how marvellous it had all been. They were terrific. Jack stood around like a melon in a butcher's shop.

At last, she swept him out of the dressing room.

'Thank God that's over,' she whispered, once they were through the curtain.

Once out on the street, and walking to the station, he said, 'I was surprised you said: you were wonderful, darling. I thought they only said that in movies.'

'What else can you say?' said Fi sharply.

'I don't know,' he said. Out of his depth now, among the luvvies.

'Sarah is in a terrible play,' she sighed. 'It's on for the next three weeks. The critics will be there in a couple of days and they will knock it for six. But I'm Sarah's friend. We went to drama school together. We're professionals in a hard world. I know what she's got to do night after night. Out there facing the audience; it's hard, I tell you. I've been in crap plays myself. I know the misery of it. It saps all your confidence. We're such weaklings, we actors. We need praise, slapping on the back, applause. That's why we're up there, under the lights. For the glory, the flowers and kisses, the raving critics. But then you hit a bummer, or even a run of bummers. And it's you and three bored people in the audience. And the only ones to support you are your fellow actors. I have to tell Sarah she's wonderful. We're in it together. This time and the next time. So she'll come to my play and tell me I am too.'

They were walking arm in arm, walking into the misty lights of the junction at the Angel.

She said, 'You have a daughter, haven't you? Haven't you ever said to her, 'You were wonderful, darling,' when she wasn't?'

Jack admitted he had.

'There you are then. It's like that. It's a tough world, and we actors have to face the brickbats. The least we can do is be nice to each other.'

'I get it,' he said. And he did. Sarah was going to have an unpleasant time the next three weeks, and her friend wasn't going to join the backstabbers. Fine. He could appreciate that.

She suddenly laughed. 'Oh, but it was awful, Jack.' She had her arm in his and was tugging at it. Jack thought of what Sarah had said about Fi's many men. He was jealous of the faceless ones, knowing this empty evening had got him nowhere. Or even shunted him out of the running.

He wanted something personal on this chilly, winter evening. To be recognised after two hours of tedium. But they were slipping downhill, into the cold fog. All they were going to talk about was the dreadful play and the ghost in room 6.

This evening wasn't going to happen. He could invite Fi out for a night under the stars with his telescope, but he knew she'd refuse. Nicely, she was good at that. Perhaps even a kiss on the cheek. No wonder she'd had a string of men.

He glanced at other couples on the glistening pavement. It must have been raining when they were inside. Some were actually laughing. How did you arrive at that state of being?

'You're quiet,' she said.

'I've run out of words. It was the most boring play I've ever been to, and I'm exhausted. I've fallen down all the snakes, not missed a single one. I'm at ground zero, empty as a balloon.' He gave a short laugh. 'I think that was the theme of the play. We're all puffed up balloons with the air leaking out.'

'If so, it's a great success,' she said. 'It's made us miserable too. What a grim twosome!'

'I think we should call it a day,' he said, hardly believing what he was saying, an attractive woman on his arm, but knowing they were going nowhere. He had no ideas how to revive it. The night was dead. 'Let's go back to Forest Gate and try something else, some other time.'

'My string of men,' sighed Fi. 'It always ends like this, you know. Though sometimes it does manage to get started.'

'And we had to clap at the end,' he said wearily. 'And then go into the dressing room and pretend.'

'We've given away all our happiness,' she said. 'And got nothing back.'

They went into Angel station, the entrance hall full of light and rumbling stairs.

On the escalator, she said, 'What do you do when you are not going to terrible plays?'

'I go out on Wanstead Flats with my telescope.'

'Do you ever go with anyone?'

'My daughter sometimes. She's good at constellations, dead hot on the craters of the moon. Occasionally a girl-friend.'

'Will you take me?'

'It might be cold and boring,' he said. 'Rainy and cloudy. And you'll wonder what you're doing there.'

'Then you'll have your revenge.'

Chapter 16

Katya was on Romford Road in her short skirt and high heels, when Johnny Potter jumped out of a taxi and slapped her round the face.

'I paid good money for you!' he yelled. 'You've hardly been out today.'

She was leaning away from him, holding her hands to her face to ward him off.

'It's cold,' she complained. 'Please don't, Johnny. I'm ill. You didn't bring my medicine.'

He grabbed her by the hair, pulled her a few yards across the pavement, then let go.

'You useless whore! Come on.'

He took her by the arm and pushed her in front of him. He was wearing a long, dark grey coat with a white silk scarf and a brown leather flat cap, and carrying a black hard case. She clipped along in her heels as he pushed her back and tight rear.

'The police came,' she wailed as she tottered along, 'I couldn't work. I tried The Chalet but they wouldn't have me. I'm ill, Johnny. Don't hit me. I do my best for you.'

'It's not good enough!' he yelled, giving her a hard shove.

They'd come into the forecourt of The Gate. There, he slowed up.

'Don't show me up now,' he said. 'Or else.'

They went in the front door. She gasped in the warm air, closing her eyes. Malik was at the desk.

'Nice to see you, Johnny,' he called as the two came along the hallway. 'It's been so quiet here. Where's all the action, I'm thinking. Though we had the police earlier.' He leaned forward, saying more intimately, 'A woman died of a heart attack in room 6.'

'The fuzz all gone?'

'Hours ago. You look cold, Katya.'

'I'm ill,' she said. 'I need my medicine. No one comes to me on nights like this.'

'She needs a warm up,' said Malik with a smirk.

'Don't we all?' said Johnny. 'Where would the world be without it?'

'Empty,' said Malik with a laugh.

'And I'd be broke.' Johnny pushed Katya forward. 'We got things to discuss. See you, Malik.'

'Don't do anything I wouldn't,' shouted Malik as they started up the stairs.

Once through the door of her room, Johnny threw Katya on the bed.

'Get 'em off,' he said, removing his coat and scarf. He kept on his bobble hat. 'Leave your shoes on. I like you in them.'

Katya quickly took off her blouse, bra and knickers. She was white and thin, except for her rounded breasts. She handed Johnny a French letter.

Johnny was quick and businesslike. She could have been any one of his girls. She happened to be Katya because Katya was here now.

'Don't you have any tissues?' he yelled in annoyance, taking a white handkerchief out of his coat pocket.

'No money,' she pleaded.

'That's because you don't work,' he yelled. 'Well, that's all going to change.'

He rapidly dressed. She took the hint and dressed too. Johnny had had the walls of the room painted in purple. Sexy, and didn't show the stains. There was a red lampshade with tassels, giving a dim light. The bed was double, the duvet and pillows bright orange. There were two wooden chairs, and by the bed a small cabinet. On top was a jug of water and a glass, plus a box of condoms.

Johnny clipped open his black case and handed Katya a twist of paper. 'Medicine. Though you don't deserve it.'

'Thank you, Johnny.'

She undid the twist and hungrily licked the powder on the paper. Her tongue filled with whiteness. She didn't swallow. With a couple of fingers she massaged her tongue and the white powder, breathing heavily as if she'd just finished a sprint.

From his case, Johnny had taken out a black box with an aerial. He put it on the floor by the bedside cabinet and plugged it in. It had a side switch which he flipped and a small light went on. He extended the aerial.

Katya was on the bed, resting against the wall, still rubbing the powder into her tongue. Her body had relaxed, and her face was slipping into a contented grin.

Johnny sat on a chair. He had a black cuff in his hands.

'You remember Sonja?' he said.

She stopped massaging and nodded, saying thickly, 'Yes.'

'Swallow that stuff,' he said. 'Talk to me properly.' He handed her a glass of water.

Katya took several swills, washing down the remnants of powder. She put down the glass.

'Sonja was a friend of yours,' he said. 'Wasn't she?' He was leaning forward, rubbing the black cuff.

'She was. I liked her very much. Can she come back?'

She was against the wall, relaxed, happy it seemed with her place in the world.

'She's been punished,' he said.

'Can she come back now?'

'She's never coming back.'

'Is she in Estonia?'

'No.' He sucked his lower lip and adjusted his leather cap. 'I have a red line. And Sonja crossed it. She robbed me. I can't have that. It sets a bad example.' He waved a finger at Katya. 'I paid good money for you. I expect a good return. I don't want you to go Sonja's way.'

'No, Johnny. I won't. I promise.'

'I know you can be a good girl. But you've got to earn money.' He leaned forward and grasped her ankle over her fishnet tights. He pulled the leg towards him. Her mouth was open, wondering what he was about to do. He opened the cuff on its hinge, then snapped it shut round her ankle.

'What's that, Johnny?'

'It's an electronic tag,' he said. 'It sends a signal to that box which sends one to my phone. Every minute a ping.' He waved a finger at her. 'But you have to stay in range. 100 metres.'

'But I can't get to the shops.'

'You don't need to go to the shops.'

'How will I eat?'

'I'll bring you food,' he said. 'I'll bring you medicine. All you have to do is work.'

'Can I take it off in the bath?'

'No,' he said. 'That's the point, you can't take it off. You're my girl. You see here?' He held her ankle, below the tag. 'It has a combination lock. So you can't get it off. If you try, I'll be very angry. But it's waterproof. So you can have a bath with it on.'

'One hundred metres,' she said. 'That's all?'

'Far enough,' he said. 'Outside the hotel and back. That's as far as you need to go. If you go out of range, I'll know at once. I won't get a ping. And I'll race over here. And what will I do?'

'Punish me.'

'I will. Very severely. Should you decide to run away, it has a GPS I can follow.' He smiled benignly. 'You see, Katya, you're my girl. Work hard and I'll bring you medicine. Run away...' He rubbed his hands together. 'You'll end up like Sonja.'

Chapter 17

As Jack walked home from Fi's, he reflected on the evening. She hadn't invited him in, he hadn't expected her to. There had been no fizz. She was attractive, he knew that objectively but the dullness of the play, those deadening two hours at the King's Head, had neutered him. He'd be first choice for guarding the Caliph's harem.

From Forest Gate station, he'd walked with Fi to her flat on Crosby Road, off the Romford Road. She'd hugged him as they were saying their goodbyes. He almost expected her to say 'you were wonderful, darling'. The booster, even when you're not. But no, she hadn't said it, that was reserved for her set, post play.

Nearly home, the chill of the evening suited him, the mist floating in the lamp heads. She'd said she'd like to come out on Wanstead Flats with his telescope. Something to say. The equivalent of 'marvellous, darling' perhaps.

'Jack!'

He looked across. Getting out of a car was Fayyad, in his long coat, as smart as ever.

'You been waiting for me?'

'I'd like a word. I was working late and popped round on the off chance. You weren't in, I was about to go, and here you are.'

'Come up for a coffee.'

They went inside, up the stairs and into Jack's flat. He was pleased to have his friend round, some company to see the night out. Jack led him into the kitchen, glad he'd had the couple of hours off this afternoon so he could clean up. It was half respectable.

'I'm going to make some Marmite on toast. Want some, Fayyad?'

'Just a coffee, mate. There'll be something for me at home, when I eventually get there.'

Jack put the kettle on and bread in the toaster. As he put the cups out and a plate, he said:

'What do you want to talk about?'

'The woman in room 6. You were there.'

'I found her, with Malik and Fi, if that's what you mean.'

Fayyad raised a placatory hand. 'It's all right, Jack. You're not under suspicion. Nothing like that. I just want to go over a few things, if you don't mind.'

'Fire away.' He took the Marmite and marge out of the fridge in readiness.

'The whole thing bothers me,' he said. 'It appears she died of a heart attack. And I have the feeling, it was meant to look that way.'

'Meaning that you don't think it was.'

'She had no ID, next to no money.'

'The door was locked from the inside,' said Jack as he spooned coffee in the cups. 'She must have locked herself in.'

'Go through getting into the room. From how you got involved. You might come up with something I've missed.'

'From the beginning, OK. I went upstairs with Malik. He told me he wanted an estimate for dividing room 6 in two. It was supposed to be empty. Which reminds me, I haven't done the estimate yet. Just went to a useless play. Don't ask me about it. I want to forget it.' He poured the hot water into the cups. 'Help yourself to milk.' Jack sat down. 'We got to the room, the two of us, and the room was locked. Malik couldn't get his key in the lock. I had a go, couldn't either. I had a look and could see the lock was blocked with a key from the inside. Malik was surprised, or at least said he was, the room was supposed to be empty.'

'Malik put Norma Jean in the room,' said Fayyad. 'He's admitted he did a deal with her. A room in exchange for sex.'

'The dirty dog.'

'But he thought that she'd left. Or that's what he says. Fi heard someone leave about 6.30. Malik told me the deal was Norma Jean would leave first thing.'

'She obviously didn't. To go on, the key was in the lock from the inside, so we couldn't get in. So I went out to my van to get a few tools.'

'How long were you away for?'

'A minute or two. When I got back up Fi had joined Malik.'

'Could Malik have done anything to the door when you were away?'

'Like what?'

The toast popped up. Jack took the slices out and buttered them.

'Don't know,' said Fayyad. 'Carry on.'

'I knocked out the key with a hammer and a screwdriver. Malik had his own key. He opened up and we went in. The inside key was on the floor, I spotted that. The room was dark, the curtains were closed. A strong smell of booze. Fi drew back the curtains and there was the woman in the bed. Dead.' Jack indicated the toast. 'You can have one of these.'

'No thanks. You eat up, Jack.' He took a sip of coffee. 'Try this for an idea. Suppose it was all set up for your benefit.'

'How do you mean?'

'Suppose Malik already knew she was dead. But he needed someone else to discover it. So he comes up with the idea of wanting to make room 6 into two rooms.'

'Each about the size of a rabbit hutch.' Jack crunched his toast and washed it down with a mouthful of coffee.

'So he invites you upstairs to look at it. And to his mock surprise, it's locked. Oh, how can that be! Please, Jack, can you get it open?'

'I agree that I was a witness. But the room was locked from the inside. How could he have done that?'

'Don't know.' He scratched his head. 'It's early days.'

'And why should he kill her, if that's what you're thinking?'

'Don't know. But the fact she had no ID – well, maybe he did know her. And he's hoping we won't find out their connection as we have no idea who she is.'

'You're jumping a lot of fences, Fayyad. And without a horse. Let's suppose he did kill her. How?'

'There'll be an autopsy, probably tomorrow.'

'All right, he does it somehow. She's in the room, dead, locked from the inside. Get round that one.'

'That is a problem. I admit it. It's all supposition, I know that. But I was hoping you could help, Jack.'

'How's that?'

'You're at the hotel, working. Have another look at room 6. See what you can come up with. And keep your ears open generally. You might see or hear things.'

'Copper's nark.'

'This could well be murder, Jack.'

'All right. I'll have another look at the room tomorrow. Say I need to check my measurements. Something like that. I'll have a listen behind curtains and look through keyholes. And report back to teacher.'

'Thanks, Jack.' Fayyad rose, buttoning his coat. 'Talk to you soon. Tomorrow is going to be a busy day.'

'I saw Hayley at Forest Gate station. She was going up to Shenfield.'

'Yes. We found a scrap of train ticket,' said Fayyad. 'Probably from Shenfield. So Hayley went there to go through the station CCTV. I heard from her about an hour ago. She thinks she's got pictures of Norma Jean going into the station.'

'Well done Hayley.'

'Must go. Don't know how the wife puts up with me.'

'Good to talk to you, mate.'

'I like chin wagging with you. It's not like with my boss. She's sharp, but she's always thinking of the money it's costing or pulling rank when I've an odd idea.'

'You could be out on a limb on this one.'

'Better to be suspicious, than to smooth everything away.'

Jack suddenly laughed.

'What's so funny?'

'Just remembered. Fi thinks there's a ghost in room 6. A woman who was murdered there in Victorian times. Maybe the ghost let Malik out, and locked up after him.'

Fayyad gave a grim smile. 'I won't try that one on the boss, thank you.'

Jack saw Fayyad to the door.

Coming back up, he thought, amazing what a bit of distraction can do. He'd forgotten the awful evening, the play and the non-event with Fi. But no one had died. Apart from the woman in room 6.

But there was something that had to be done tomorrow. Apart from looking at the room for Fayyad. Much, much more important. The imperative had been delivered several times. The cello was still in his van. In the morning, before anything else, he must get rid of it. He wrote a note on a scrap of paper: CELLO! And put it in the middle of the kitchen table held down by a cup. He would see it first thing and be unable to ignore its command.

Tomorrow then, have another look at the room. Be Fayyad's ears and eyes in the hotel. Maybe suggest another date with Fi. If that was a runner. With all her other men.

Sufficient unto the day are the troubles thereof, as his mother said too often. Wake up to the first day of the rest of your life, as they said at Alcohol Halt. Tomorrow is another day. All this Christmas cracker stuff. New sunrise, new beginning. Ra Ra!

To which, some cynic would add: same old face, same old body, in the same old clothes.

So what did she think of him? A dull stick. No fizz, no buzz, no bang. So why was he so dejected? Because he'd expected so much more from the evening. Been excited at the thought of a visit to the theatre with an attractive actress.

More fool you, Jack Bell.

At least he was home and warm, with his Marmite on toast. OK, he was a dull stick. No getting away from it. A Jack of All Trades grubbing for work around Forest Gate. A night out on the Flats with his telescope registered as a high point. Whereas she'd had three weeks on *EastEnders*. Almost a star. Though she was then relegated to an ugly sister at the Hackney Empire.

He laughed at the thought of Fi taking a custard pie in the face at the Hackney Empire.

But custard washes off. Tomorrow is another day. Ra Ra! He should do an evening class. Learn about plays and books and paintings. All the arty stuff in the world. Instead of being limited to bricks and wood and cement.

Chapter 18

The note on the table screamed at him, as it was supposed to. He'd been carting that cello around all day yesterday. Today, like the desired object in a fantasy, it had to be got to Mordor or he would shrivel in the sorcerer's glare. And the world would be overrun by orcs, Daleks or zombies. Or all three in brief harmony, before they set to eating each other to the last munching mouth, which would then consume itself.

If he didn't deliver the cello.

First stop, no nonsense, not to The Gate Hotel, but to Sebert Road. Fortunately he was ahead of the school run. Even had the rarity of a nearby parking spot.

Mia opened the door in the white shirt and navy trousers of her school uniform.

'At last!' she exclaimed. 'You've made a right fool of me, Dad.'

'Well, you never expected anything different,' he said handing over the instrument.

'The Head of Music was chasing me all day, then the cello teacher and Mum was phoning... And what could I say, but my Dad had it and kept saying he would bring it in. And he didn't.'

'Sorry.'

His daughter had a piece of toast in one hand and a phone in the other. Acrobatically, she managed to take in the cello, then put it down, without dislodging either.

He had transferred ownership. At last.

'I'd told the Head of Music we should get a quartet together,' said Mia. 'She said, Good idea, Mia. And she got four of us together at lunch time. It was your idea, your suggestion.'

'Was it?'

'Yes, in the van, going into school. The best idea you've had in ages.'

'Thank you.'

'Not thank you. You shamed me. There were the four of us, three with their instrument. And one without. A viola, two violins and a blank that was me.'

'Well, you've got it now. I'm sorry. It was an eventful day.'

'So was mine. You're not the only alive person in Forest Gate.'

'I'm not going to say sorry to you any more. I think I've said it three times. So say hello to your Mum for me and I'll see you on Thursday at the concert.'

'I'll be dreadful. Under rehearsed for the orchestra. And the quartet will all blame me for the lack of time together...'

'Who's that at the door, Mia?' Alison came out of the kitchen. 'Ah, you, Jack. Finally got the message. Sixth time of asking. Par for the course, I'd say.'

'Leave him alone,' said Mia. 'He brought it back, didn't he?'

'Eventually,' she said stretching out the syllables.

'It was my fault,' said Mia puffing herself up. 'I shouldn't have left it in the van. My cello, my fault. Nuff said. Game over. Let's finish breakfast. See you Thursday, Dad.'

He wanted to say, Wonderful, darling. But figured that would cause an outbreak of astonishment.

Instead he said, 'Break a leg. Not a string.'

'Ha ha,' said Mia poking out her tongue as she closed the door on him.

Jack breathed a sigh of relief. Job done. Without too much recrimination. First Mia had attacked him, then when Alison joined in she had defended him. Wonderful, darling, he said to himself as he got back in the van and drove to work.

Chapter 19

Fi was cooking in the hotel kitchen. Eggs were in the pan and on the hot plate, sausages sizzling, bacon crisping, beans on low as toast popped. Her hair was in her Rosie the Riveter scarf as she conducted the breakfast orchestra, slice in hand.

She was putting plates of breakfast on the trolley when Geela entered, in green shalwar kameez and matching hijab. She took a plate of egg on toast and beans off the trolley.

'Hey, you can't have those!' yelled Fi, waving the slice.

'I can have what I want in my own kitchen.'

Fi pointed outside. 'Those guys have to get to work. That one's an order. You can't just grab what you want off the trolley.'

'I am not a kitchen girl to be ordered about by you.'

Fi shook her slice. 'Eat it then. But those eggs were fried with bacon.'

Geela dropped the plate, which smashed, scattering the eggs, beans and toast about the floor.

'Now look what you made me do!'

'I made you! Lord God save me. I am trying to run a kitchen here. Feed the guests, who've got to get to work. And you rush in and take one of my orders... Look at that mess! Who's going to clean it up?'

'If you didn't yell at me, I wouldn't drop it.'

'Me! It was you.'

Geela came towards Fi, waving her finger like a deadly weapon.

'All the trouble here comes from you.'

And she skidded on egg, throwing her arms high and wide to try to stop herself, failing and tumbling over backwards into the jettisoned breakfast.

Fi couldn't control a smirk.

'You whore!' yelled Geela, on her back in the egg and beans. 'Sleeping with my husband. Ordering me around in the kitchen... Laughing at me. I will not have it.'

'I am not sleeping with your husband, Geela.'

'Mrs Bashir to you! I am your employer.'

Geela was getting off the ground, her hands sticky as Malik came into the kitchen.

'What's going on here? The guests are waiting for breakfast.'

'Mrs Bashir just grabbed a plate,' exclaimed Fi, 'dropped it and fell on her butt.' She couldn't stop herself grinning, putting a hand to her mouth to stop it developing into a laugh.

'See how she treats me?' yelled Geela, wiping her hands on a tea towel. 'The woman you are sleeping with.'

'Sh! Sh!' whispered Malik, pointing to the outside. 'Don't yell to the world.' He put a finger to his lips and continued. 'How many times do I have to say it, I am not sleeping with Fi.'

'So why the perfume on your shirt?'

'Why on earth would I wear perfume to work?' exclaimed Fi, clamping her hands to her head. 'To cook and change sheets. Scent! What – Eau de Pantry!'

Malik was pointing outside, a finger to his lips.

'Shut up, you slut,' hissed Geela. She turned to her husband. 'So whose scent was it, if not this half caste's?'

Malik hesitated, blew out his cheeks, then said, 'Must we have this conversation here and now, with guests waiting for breakfast?'

'Whose scent was it? Tell me?'

Malik looked about him as if there might be an escape. Fi and Geela were waiting on him.

'One of the whores,' he said with a shrug. 'Just once. Late. You know how it is.'

Geela threw the tea cloth at him.

'You are disgusting.' And she swept from the room.

Fi was looking up at the ceiling, trying to control her breathing. Malik had got down and begun wiping the floor with the tea cloth.

'I can't stand this,' said Fi.

'It won't be much longer,' he said, grimacing at the stickiness.

'How much longer?'

'Soon, soon. We must give it a few weeks. Let the fuss die down.'

He rose and came to her, putting a hand on her shoulder. 'I'll go out and speak to the guests. And take this trolley, it'll keep some of them happy. You do your best, Fi, I'll do the apologising.'

'Right,' she said, wiping the back of her hand over her eyes. 'Eggs, bacon, beans, automatic pilot. Get out there, Malik. Keep them sweet. I'll hustle along. And don't let that cockroach of a wife come back in here. Or I swear, I'll smack her with a frying pan.'

Malik scampered out with the trolley.

Chapter 20

The area he'd dug out yesterday was more or less level. Better than Jack had hoped when he'd left off last night, cold and working in semi darkness. Roughly a foot deep. It didn't have to be exact, as gravel and sand were to go in and could make up any discrepancy before the final layer of cement.

There was a heated argument in the kitchen. Fi's voice, Geela and someone else quieter, probably Malik. Yes, it was him, though his words were indistinct. Through the lounge window, he could see seven or so guests at the tables watching the kitchen door, catching some of the row, waiting for breakfast.

Not a happy family, but not his concern. Though maybe it was, if he was to be Fayyad's nark. He was more than curious, hearing Geela yell out 'whore!'. That could only be addressed to one person. Amazing that Fi stayed, though jobs to fit in with her acting weren't easy to find. And it was close by. All the advantages. But then, Geela? All the disadvantages.

He'd no doubt get three versions. All the hard-done-by people. Who was doing what to whom.

There are distinct advantages to working on your own. No one to belittle you, no rows. No other worker to complain when you made a mistake as everyone did. No arguments about who was working hardest, or about money. Always about money.

Two people on a job, a partnership, was like a marriage. Could work, could be hell. Three meant two could gang up against one. Geela wanted Fi out, that was obvious. Who would Malik side with?

Whichever one he was talking to. Maybe the two women should get together and oust him.

Was any of this useful to pass onto Fayyad? Maybe, maybe not. If Norma Jean had killed herself, nothing was. Though if she was killed, who hated whom most would count. Unless the ghost did it. Which might count as suicide until Fi took the witness stand.

Enough.

Jack put on the ear protectors to end the row. Starting his machine killed it for the diners too. They were eating though, no doubt giving their thoughts on the kitchen ruckus. Jack checked everything was in working order, making sure the arm went up and down, the bucket turned as it should. A minute or so of this satisfied him that he and the machine were in sync, and he headed off. Along the car park, past the cars and through the arch, with the arm kept low to get through.

There were many loads of gravel and sand to be ferried today. So much easier if he could have had them tipped by the workings, straight from the truck. But a truck couldn't get under the arch. So the gravel and sand were out front, and had to be brought to the back.

The Betelgeuse was a trusty little bus. Though if it packed up on him, with the strain on the small engine – not unlikely, he'd either have to hire one himself or hump the gravel and sand by wheelbarrow. Like building Stonehenge single handed.

That was the disadvantage of working on your own.

With a knife, Jack sliced down the sides of one of the cubical gravel sacks. The released gravel slipped out into a heap. There was going to be a lot of cleaning up when he'd done. But that was another day's worry. For now, he had to get the stuff from A to B and hope he'd got the quantities right.

No one else to blame.

Jack took a full scoop of gravel in the digger bucket and headed back, adjusting the arm as he came through the arch. This would be second nature after half a dozen trips but for now he had to concentrate, taking it step by step. Already he was getting chilled, without a cab and little action to keep him warm. He'd work as long as he could take it, and hope Fi would bring out coffee in a while. If she was speaking to him as they'd parted somewhat coldly.

He looked up at the sky. The sun was shining, but it was that illusory winter sunshine with little heat in it. Good for the stars though. A clear sky. If it stayed that way, then out tonight on the Flats with the telescope. Fi had said she wanted to come but that could have been appeasing words for a bad play. Assume she's not, then he wouldn't be disappointed.

Work. The sky won't go away.

At his workings, he brought the arm down and turned the bucket; the contents tipped out into a small pyramid of gravel. One! He slapped the engine for luck, and headed back out to refill the bucket. There was a chilly wind. The big earth movers had warm cabs and surround sound. But would cost a month's salary to hire for a day.

And wouldn't fit under the arch anyway.

Over the next forty minutes, Jack went to and fro, ferrying gravel to his workings. The cold seeped in with each traverse, finger tips going blue, feet turning to blocks of ice. He could take no more. Jack turned off the machine. That could do with a break too. He warmed his hands on the engine, rubbing his palms together and stomping his feet.

Having rubbed some heat in, he put on a pair of rough gloves and began raking the gravel. It wasn't all here yet, but warming up was a priority. He raked the tops off the heaps, drawing them together. The spirit level would come out later, once he had all the gravel on the site.

Motion, heat.

He was still raking when the smokers came out. The two guys were holding hands, released as they settled on chairs. Clem began rolling a joint. They had items of colour about their suits, a cravat, a lapel pin. Clem, Jack noted, had odd socks, one yellow, one red, just showing at the hem of his trousers. Maybe that was the new fashion, until he noticed the other guy had the same colour socks. A love token or a befuddled mistake as they'd dressed.

'Digging holes and filling them in again,' said Clem usefully.

'I do a lot of that,' said Jack.

'Don't we all,' said his pal.

Clem said, as he rolled the papers round the tobacco and resin, 'You caused some controversy yesterday.'

'How did I do that?' said Jack, stopping raking.

'The marketing symposium I was at. There's a big word for you.'

'It just means conference,' said his pal.

Jack was irked. Pen pushers assuming if you worked with your hands you were dumb. He'd been to an astronomy symposium organised by his favourite mag. Conference, speakers, audio visual.

Stay cool.

'I told them I'd seen this builder called Jack of All Trades,' went on Clem. 'And that started them off. A ding dong on whether it was a good or bad name.'

'What did they settle on?' said Jack leaning on the rake.

'Mixed reception,' said Clem, handing the unlit joint to his mate. 'Some thought it good. A joke in the name. Some thought it bad, condemning yourself with your brand name. I reminded them they were all talking about it. And they argued about that too. Whether all publicity was good publicity.'

'What do you advise?' said Jack going back to raking the gravel.

'Scrap it,' said Clem. 'Employ me to come up with a new name, logo, and graphic concept.'

'Don't listen to him,' said his mate, taking in a long drag. 'You don't want his fancy pals getting hold of you. They'll mess you around for six months, charge you a fortune, then come up with something like Walter of All Works and a dancing ladder logo.'

Jack laughed. The resin wafting in the air, the two men's faces had softened.

'But my name's Jack,' he said. 'Not Walter. And my ladders had better not dance.'

'Immaterial,' said Clem waving the joint. 'All advertising is 90 per cent lies.'

'99 percent,' insisted his mate. 'And that's on a good day after lunch.'

'Do you two always argue?' said Jack.

'Not as much as they do in there,' said Clem with a whistle, indicating the kitchen window. 'That was hammer and tongs.'

'And cold food,' said his pal.

'This is the noisiest hole I've ever been to,' said Clem with a chuckle. 'And I've been to some, I can tell you. Take a tip. Don't stay here if you want to sleep. Last night we had a roomful of junkies next door playing Radiohead all night.'

'And the night before, we had a screaming threesome,' joined in his mate.

'They were loud,' exclaimed Clem. 'One of them was that woman who died. You know about that?'

'I did hear,' said Jack, immediately clued into what Clem had said, and not wanting to go into details of what he knew. 'Who were the threesome?'

'There was Malik. He's a horny so and so. There was the woman, the one who died. At least I assumed it was her. In room 6 anyway where she died. And there was Fi, you know the cook.'

'Fi? You sure?'

His mate said, 'Clem couldn't be sure of anything. He was nine tenths cut.'

'I'd know Malik's voice anywhere,' Clem insisted. 'And I'm pretty sure it was Fi. The walls are paper thin. And we were just next door. I'd bet you on Fi.'

'A tenner,' said his mate.

'You're on.'

They shook hands and Jack went back to raking. Two stoned guys would make lousy witnesses. He'd believe it of Malik, he'd make up a threesome at the drop of a hat. But Fi? He couldn't believe it of her. Maybe one of the whores. Doing what they were paid for.

He started up the machine, to get away from the two pals going on about the threesome, suggesting a tag match, acrobatics, ring a ring of roses, blind man's buff. Jack drove off to get another load. When he'd returned with a full bucket, Fi was there handing out coffee. He turned off the machine and she handed him a steaming mug.

'Thanks,' he said. 'I need this.'

'Big row in the kitchen,' said Clem to Fi.

'Tell me about it,' she said, not willing to expand.

'Cold food,' said his mate. 'Eggs congealed on the plate.'

'I'm sorry,' she said. 'It got rather out of hand.' She turned to Jack. 'There's some toast and scrambled egg if you fancy it, Jack.'

'Sure,' he said. 'Be glad of a fill up.'

And he followed her inside.

Chapter 21

She settled him at the kitchen table and gave him scrambled egg on toast.

'The tea is stewed, I'm afraid.'

'So long as it's warm,' he said.

'I hardly know what I'm doing this morning. It so shakes me up when she comes in all guns blazing. I lose track. I wonder the point of it.'

She poured him a mug of tea, and then went out with the trolley to collect crockery. The egg was cold, the toast too. If he'd been served this in a café he wouldn't have come back. Hearing her busy in the dining hall, he scraped the egg into the bin. The toast was OK. A minute or so later she was back, the trolley piled high with dirty crockery.

'All this waste,' she exclaimed, indicating the sausages, beans and egg on the plates. 'A row in the kitchen and this is what you end up with.' She scraped waste into the bin. Her arms were bare, wearing rubber gloves, her hair tied in an efficient scarf.

'Did you manage the egg?' she said.

'No.'

'The cook always gets it,' she said. 'I should've put it in the microwave. Sorry. But I'm so het up. I've got to calm down. Geela always gets me like this.'

'The toast is OK,' he said.

'You mean it's not burnt. Have some marmalade.' She passed him two tiny jars.

'A bit of marmalade always sweetens the toast,' he said as he smeared it on.

Lots better, as he crunched it. The tea was stewed, but he'd been warned. Builders can't be too fussy, considering some of the dishwater he'd drunk in mess huts.

He was watching her. Fi had slowed down, the row had definitely got to her. She was putting plates in the dishwasher, bending and swinging from trolley to dishwasher, hips and backside swaying, bringing him back to the threesome in room 6. The noise and acrobatics. Could he ask her if she'd been there? What would she say? 'Mind your own business', or throw a pot at him.

It was burning in him. Was she or wasn't she there? A tincture of jealousy and curiosity. And then there was the woman who died, said to be involved too. Dare he ask her?

He said, 'Those gay guys were talking about you.'

She turned to him, dirty plates in hand.

'And what have they added to my besmirched reputation?'

He hesitated. He could just come out with it, he was only saying what they'd said. But what right did he have?

'They wonder why you stay here.'

'Me too,' she said, as she filled the dishwasher shelves with cups and plates. 'It's fine when Geela's not in. I just get on with things. But when she's in, I know there's going to be a bust up. I wait for it. And it always comes. Could be out of anything. The other day, she brought in a mustard pot I'd forgotten on a table. Made a big thing of it. Another time I left a bin in the hall upstairs. It was empty, it wasn't like it was full of rubbish. I'd have put it back in the room as soon as I went up again. But it was enough to get her started. There's always something. Bound to be. There's only one of me.' Her eyes were welling. 'What's wrong with the woman!' She slammed the dishwasher door and set the machine going. 'Enough of the cow.' She snapped off her rubber gloves, throwing them by the sink. 'Bring your tea upstairs. I want to show you room 6.'

He followed her out. It was as if she'd snapped out of it as the rubber gloves came off. She scampered quickly up the stairs, he couldn't keep up with her with the mug in his hand. By the time he got to the landing, she'd gone into the room, leaving the door ajar. He entered. The bed was unmade, the duvet thrown back, stains on the sheets.

'A couple were here last night,' she said. 'I saw them this morning. The girl was way too young, I'm sure. The man more than twice her age. Malik doesn't ask questions. Just takes the money.'

There were tissues and condoms in a full bin, an empty rum bottle poking out, like the remnant of a shipwreck.

Jack went to the window. Sunlight was coming in, traffic rumbling by on the main road.

'We're not here for the view,' she said. 'Come here.' And led him under the ceiling rose. 'Stay right there.' She went to the door and closed it. 'Don't talk for a minute. Just feel. Don't look at me. Just feel.'

Not his strongest suit, Alison had told him. Still, she'd been angry, and angry wives fling all sorts, true or otherwise. Jack closed his eyes, unsure whether he was supposed to, and listened. Feel, was the instruction. His hands along his thighs, his tongue in his mouth, feet on the ground, the hum of traffic, water gurgling in a pipe, footsteps somewhere overhead, a country and western song somewhere. Was it Hank Williams? What was Fi doing? Watching him or in her own space? Mia would have cello practice today... He was drifting, he should be feeling. A door slammed somewhere, footsteps on the stairs. You'd need earplugs to sleep in this room. A room where a woman had died, following a three-some which Fi may or may not have been part of. And last night occupied by a couple who got drunk and had sex, probably illegally. Feel the energy. Concentrate. Eyelids, lips pressed together, a gurgle in his stomach. Fi thinks the place is haunted, some woman murdered a long time ago. But he couldn't feel her at all. The constant traffic, a creak somewhere, shouting in the road outside. Hank Williams unhappy about someone.

How much longer? This wasn't doing anything for him. He needed to get back to work.

'Open your eyes.'

Jack did so, grateful to stop feeling though he knew he hadn't been much good at it. She was a couple of metres away, crossed arms clutching her shoulders as if protecting herself.

'Did you feel it?' she said.

'You mean the ghost?'

'Yes. Or anything.'

'No.'

'Don't you feel a chill in the room?' She leaned forward, appealing with her hands. He wanted to oblige. 'Maybe a presence?' she went on, pressing him for something. 'Don't you feel you are being watched?'

'No.'

'Nothing?' She was staring at him, obviously disappointed. 'Nothing at all?'

'Nothing. What did you feel?'

'I saw her,' she exclaimed. 'While you were standing there with your eyes closed. A Victorian woman walked across the room, a brown dress down to her ankles. She gave you a sharp push. You were in her way. Didn't you feel it?'

'No.'

'Why me!' she cried. 'Why can I see it and no one else can?' Her hands were shaking, she was looking about her feverishly. 'She's watching us. She wants me to do something. And I can't. I must get out of here. I will not be her tool.'

Fi ran from the room, flapping her arms as if to ward off a swarm of bees. She slammed the door after her. Jack looked about the room. A messy room after the guests had left. He sat on the arm of the armchair. He certainly had no feeling for whatever Fi had claimed to see. Was it simply overactive imagination? Or his insensitivity?

There was no ghost.

The room was grubby, a smell of booze and sweat, the bed unmade. The mess of a space where each night new guests take over to maybe sleep, have sex, take drugs, listen to music, watch TV. Leave their debris for the cleaner.

Except, he recalled, there'd been little mess when they'd found the body. The room was clean apart from the whisky bottle by the bed. The bin empty, Norma had next to nothing herself, apart from the clothes she'd been wearing and a handbag. And yet there'd been a threesome in this room according to the gay guys.

If so, someone had tidied the room.

PART THREE:
FARADAY'S CAGE

Chapter 22

Jack went back to work. He continued bringing over the gravel with Betelgeuse for the next half hour, and then set to raking. All the gravel was in place; it had to be levelled and firmed. The sun was shining and he was warm with work. Very basic work, layer to go on layer like a sandwich cake.

The smokers had gone while he'd been away, and he was content to be alone. No one to argue with, to say things which he had no way of challenging. Creating scandal for the sake of it. Or asking him to feel the presence of something he couldn't see.

There were no clouds. Little wind to blow any in. If it held out, the night would be made for stargazing. Cold winter nights were the darkest, the sun way below the horizon, whereas in midsummer the nights were short, the afterglow of sunset caught too soon by the coming dawn. He owed it to himself, after the boredom of last night, to go out on Wanstead Flats with his telescope. To set it up in the centre, as far away from houses and street lights as he could get. There was always light pollution in town, the best he could do was minimise it by going to the darkest area he could find. He had filters which caught some light pollution, but there was always less detail than you'd see from a moor or up a mountain. Even so, there were planets and nebulae to explore, if the cloud enemy made a temporary retreat.

Fi came out the French windows, carrying a sandwich on a plate. She looked perkier, her sleeves rolled up.

'For you. A bacon sandwich,' she said. 'To make up for a poor breakfast.'

'You didn't have to,' he said, taking the sandwich. It was warm and greasy, the flesh pink and crinkly. 'Delicious,' he murmured after the first bite, the salty heat flowing into him.

'I have to make it up to you, after the terrible play. I can't give you a terrible breakfast too. What would you think of me?'

'This hits the spot,' exclaimed Jack. He kissed her on the cheek.

She twisted round and kissed him on the mouth.

'All bacony,' she murmured.

Jack let the rake fall, putting the sandwich on the engine. This was the embrace that couldn't happen last night between two zombies. He pressed into her warmth, massaging her back, resting cheek on cheek as if they were the last dancers on the floor, each holding the other up.

Gently, she ushered him away. 'Someone might come,' she whispered.

'Is Geela still about?' he gestured to the window, aware of the silly smile on his face.

'She's gone,' she said, smiling too. 'Thank heaven for that. I'm just here for another twenty minutes and then I have to sprint to my rehearsal.'

'Would you like to see the moon tonight?'

'Have you a space rocket?'

'No, a telescope. If it stays this clear, it'll be a beautiful night to see the stars. Nowhere fancy. I can't give you the crystal skies of Mauna Kea or the Andes. ' He laughed. 'Just Wanstead Flats.'

'Don't fancy the Andes,' she said with a shrug. 'Cold up there. And what was the other one?'

'Mauna Kea. An extinct volcano on Hawaii. Famous for its dark skies.'

'If it's famous, why haven't I heard of it?'

'In astronomy circles,' he said.

She laughed. 'Don't mix in them.'

'Me neither. But Wanstead Flats... We might see Orion's nebula.'

'No one has promised me that before.'

'Not one of your many men?'

Fi poked out her tongue. 'Don't believe Sarah's mischief. I must go. See you this evening. I've got to finish here. And run to my rehearsal.'

She darted in and kissed him on the cheek, and before he could say anything, she was through the French windows.

Jack picked up the remnants of the sandwich. Cold but tasty. He felt his cheek where she'd kissed him. It had come out of the blue. Warmth. The exchange. The promise. Tonight on the Flats.

He finished the sandwich, gazing through the window of the lounge. No sign of her. She'd be racing from room to room with sheets and a vacuum cleaner, then off to her rehearsal. She never stopped.

Jack went back to raking, barely aware of what he was doing, inventing possibilities, making futures. All the tease and fluff brought on by a kiss. He was a sucker for invention, wanting someone to share his life. To be there in the dead of night. Even a woman who believed in ghosts. He'd even accept fairies. She didn't see them everywhere, all the time, poking their heads out. Boo!

But that threesome? Surely not. But he couldn't kill the thought. Sarah's 'You and your men, Fi'. But she wouldn't have been in room 6, not with Malik and Norma Jean. He couldn't believe it. He argued back and forth as he raked the gravel for the next half hour. And then, with the digger, rode over the area to press it firm, so that it wouldn't sink over time and crack the concrete.

He came off the workings with Betelgeuse and checked the level with a plank and spirit level. Fine. Yesterday's interruption had put him behind, but today was going well.

Next a layer of sand. Once that was done, he'd put in the wooden forms for concreting tomorrow.

This was to be a parking area. He had to build up the layers so they would take the weight of vehicles, with a slight incline so it wouldn't puddle in wet weather.

He'd promised to have another look at room 6 for Fayyad. He'd been in there with Fi, but had his eyes closed most of the time. This time, eyes open. Quite what he was expecting... Nothing much, just a way Malik could get out of the room, having killed Norma Jean, but not through the door as it was locked, with the key on the inside. Through the walls perhaps, hanging on to the ghost's coat-tails.

That would satisfy Fi. Probably not Fayyad.

Get started on the sand, then up to room 6. See if he could assist Fayyad one way or another. Though those smokers talking about the party next door... The threesome intrigued him. Malik being one of them. He'd accept that, as Malik had already admitted to having sex with Norma. But they'd also said Fi was there. Can't be true. She had to be here, working, by six!

Another woman. Who? That whore, what was her name?

Jack drove the digger out, through the arch, to the sacks of sand. Remnants of gravel were lying about. He bulldozed it into a heap, against the wall, out of the way. It was waste now. Not much, fairly well calculated. Let's hope the sand worked out as well.

Jack sliced the fabric of a sand sack, the amber particles slid into a long dune. He took a handful and rubbed it in between his fingers. It was dry and grainy. Be easy to rake, make a good bed for the concrete.

Katya came out of the main door. She was stumbling and weeping, and collapsed on the top step, her face in her hands.

Jack went to her, wiping the grit off his fingers.

'What's wrong?'

Katya looked up, tears streaking her make up, thick lipstick cracked at the corners. She wiped a thin hand over her eyes, the nails purple and fake.

She said, 'Johnny is going to kill me.'

'Johnny who?'

'Potter,' she exclaimed. 'Look!' She stretched out a leg in fishnets, and pointed out the cuff round her ankle above her red, high-heeled shoe.

'An electronic tag,' said Jack, puzzled. He'd seen one before on a man he knew who was on probation. He looked closer. 'It's got a combination lock. Johnny Potter put this on?'

'I can go one hundred metres,' she said sniffing. 'Any further, even to get a sandwich, and he'll be over here. And beat me.'

'You must go to the police,' he said. 'This is slavery.'

'No, no,' she threw her hands up, 'never the police.'

Jack was thinking, who if not. It had to be the police.

'The police are the right people,' he said. 'Believe me, Katya.'

'Not the police. I will never go to the police. They no help at all.'

'OK,' he said. 'I get the message. No cops. Let me have a think.'

He strolled about biting his lower lip, looking at the tag. She didn't want the cops, maybe she was illegal. Been badly treated by them before, perhaps. And there was Tosser Potter. His old school mate, hardly mate. Her pimp, restricting her to 100 metres. It was slavery. What to do? It came to him. Alison. She was on the management committee of a women's refuge. This was her realm.

Katya wailed, 'He's going to kill me. Like that woman the other night. I know he will. She had a tag.'

'What woman?'

'The dead one,' exclaimed Katya. 'In room 6. She had a tag. Like me. Now she's dead.'

'She didn't,' he said, confused.

'She did,' Katya insisted. 'We had a party. I saw it.'

'The night she died?'

'Yes. Please help me.' She clutched his wrists. 'Or Johnny will kill me. I know he will.' Her hands flew to her face. 'I am his prisoner. Like a chicken waiting to have its throat cut.'

Jack bent down to her level, so he could look her in the eye. He was about to put a hand on her knee but the short skirt and fishnets stopped him. Too sexual. He clamped his hands to his thighs.

'I know someone who has contacts,' he said. 'We'll get you to a safe house.'

'What about this thing?' she said, pointing to the tag. 'It has GPS. He'll find me wherever I go.'

'I'll sort that out,' he said, his mind ticking over rapidly. How can you cut out electronic signals? An electrician had shown him once, a Faraday cage, telling him shoplifters used them. It would quite likely work. He needed some bits and pieces.

'I must get back to work,' she exclaimed, standing up, straightening her fishnets and skirt. She clutched his hand. 'Please help me. I will only be out the front here. I can't go further, just there and to my room with a punter. Find me a safe place, please.'

'I'll phone around,' he said. 'Right away. Go to work or he'll be suspicious.'

'Thank you, Jack.'

She squeezed his hand and walked away, down the drive and out onto the street. She must be so cold, in that short skirt and tights. The least of her troubles. He took out his phone and scrolled to Alison. He pressed dial.

'Jack,' she said.

'There's a woman here who thinks she's going to be killed.'

'She must go to the police.'

'She refuses,' he said. 'I don't know why. She's got an electronic tag on her. She needs somewhere safe.'

He explained what he knew about tags and about Johnny Potter. Adding that a woman with a tag had been killed the night before last.

'It's a police matter,' insisted Alison.

'She won't go to them,' said Jack. 'I told her to. I would have taken her. But she won't go to the cops. Maybe in a safe house she can be persuaded.'

'OK,' said Alison after a pause. 'I'll have to cancel an appointment. But she takes priority. I'll make some phone calls. Get her ready to go.'

'Thanks,' said Jack.

Alison closed the call.

Jack looked out at Katya on the pavement outside the hotel. She was talking to a man in a car, leaning forward, her leather skirt six inches above her knees, a rip in the tights on a thigh. He turned away, he had things to do. He drove the digger back to his site without a load. So it was Katya in the room with Malik and the woman. Not Fi. He knew it couldn't be Fi. Just as well he hadn't put it to her. Katya. And Norma Jean had a tag on. Who put it there?

Other thoughts for other times. He Googled on his phone, 'Faraday Cage', and read rapidly. A lot of it was too technical for him. But he had the gist of it after a few articles and a discussion group. Work was on hold. Get Katya ready. He went through the French windows, into the lounge. No one was about. Then quickly into the kitchen. Fi had gone; it was empty, everything cleared up. He grabbed a roll of kitchen foil and went through the cupboards, finding a couple of large wire strainers. They would have to serve.

He set off to his van to improvise.

Chapter 23

Fayyad and Hayley were in DS Nikki Martin's office. The senior officer was behind her desk while Hayley brought her up to date, showing the pictures on her laptop that she'd grabbed from the CCTV images.

'That's her,' said DS Martin comparing the image on the laptop to the photos on her desk. 'And yes, that bag is distinctive. Strange though, isn't it? She's going to a hotel in Forest Gate but takes no luggage.'

'She's running away,' said Fayyad.

'Seems likely,' said DS Martin. 'No time to pack.' She turned to Hayley. 'You say you've had a response?'

'Yes, ma'am. I put a poster up in Shenfield station. And then thought, why did she go specifically to Forest Gate? I had another poster with me. And so I put that one up in Forest Gate station. Twenty minutes ago a woman phoned me. A Forest Gate woman. She thinks Norma Jean is her sister.'

'Did she say any more?'

'She told me her sister was living in Shenfield. I didn't press for more details. I thought I'd talk to you first, ma'am. But I told her we'd be over to see her shortly.'

'Then off you go, Hayley. See if the woman is Norma Jean's sister. The Shenfield connection makes it very likely. If she makes the right noises, then take her to the mortuary for an identification.'

'The autopsy is today,' said Fayyad. 'I'd like to go along.'

DS Nikki Martin tapped her desk with her fingers. 'We have no evidence that this is a suspicious death, Fayyad. Just

116

an unknown woman dead in a hotel room. No weapon, the room was locked from the inside.'

'We think she was running away,' he said. 'She had no ID or money. It smells of suspicious circumstances.'

'So it's all down to your nose, Fayyad. While *I* might accept that as a reason for expenditure, others, less familiar with your nose, might bridle.'

Hayley had switched off her laptop and had risen.

'I'll be off, ma'am.'

'Phone through after you've spoken to the putative sister. You know what we need. Norma Jean's real name, address, next of kin, anything you might think relevant.'

'Yes, ma'am.'

And Hayley was away.

DS Nikki Martin leaned back, rubbing her chin. Fayyad knew better than to push further, but... If Norma Jean had suffered a heart attack, then no more expense was justified, beyond getting the body identified. The Shenfield squad could contact next of kin. All done and dusted. Unless there was foul play.

'Why no ID on her?' he said. 'That bothers me.'

'Perhaps she didn't bring any, on purpose.'

'But no money, ma'am. Not even a credit card.'

'Could be suicide.'

'No sign of it. And why go to Forest Gate to do it?'

'Because she wouldn't be interrupted in a hotel,' said DS Martin.

'But she has a sister here.'

'Might have. Don't presume. But OK, for argument's sake, let's say it is her sister. But Norma Jean locked herself in, Fayyad. Get out of that one.'

'Suppose something was done to her before she went in the room?'

'Like what?'

He thought, grasping. 'Poison. Something slow acting.'

His boss took a deep breath. 'You're fishing in a shallow puddle, Fayyad. But I suppose there's the off chance... All right, go to the autopsy. But unless we come up with something tangible between you and Hayley, this case is done with.'

Chapter 24

Jack was at work on his small workbench, by his van, the side door open so he could get to his tools. He hoped Malik wouldn't come out and ask what he was doing with kitchen foil and cut up food strainers. Though he hadn't seen him around. Maybe upstairs fiddling the books.

He had no idea how long Alison would be, and he'd have to catch Katya between punters. First though, he had to make the Faraday cage or Johnny would be after Katya, and him too as he'd be with her. His van would be no match for Johnny's car if the Faraday cage didn't block the signal from the tag.

With wire cutters, Jack cut off the strainer mesh from the metal it was attached to. Then he cut a hole in the bottom of the mesh, so Katya's leg would fit through. There were two strainers. He did the same to the other and then stuck the two of them together with gaffer tape, making a sort of bulging tube of mesh. He cut up the side, so it could fit round her leg. He wrapped the mesh tube in foil.

Now to test it.

Jack had a spare phone in his dashboard compartment. A cheap thing he used occasionally if he'd forgotten his main phone. Jack got it out and switched it on. Fortunately, it had enough battery. He put it in his makeshift cage.

Jack dialled the spare with his everyday phone and waited. Nothing. He dialled again. Nothing. And a third time. It seemed no signal was getting through. So far, so good. But he must make sure.

Jack took the spare phone out of the cage and dialled it with his usual phone. The spare rang. He was triumphant.

His bodge job worked; it had cut out the phone signal. And that was what the tag would send: a GPS signal via a phone network. Cut it off and Johnny would have no idea where Katya was. Or where he was, along with her.

Jack tidied the debris away, throwing it deep into the van, just in case Malik should come out and catch him at it. Clean it up later. Now he had to wait for Alison to call.

It was hard to concentrate, this was a risky business. For Katya and for him too. Johnny was dangerous. But nothing would happen until he got Alison's call. Not knowing how long she'd be, he went back to work, carting sand over with Betelgeuse and dumping it on the gravel base. No one had seen him working on the Faraday cage, and even if they had they wouldn't know what he'd been up to.

As he dumped sand in his workings, he considered what he must do. Katya must be got away quickly. He'd cage her tag. It would stop sending any signals but Johnny would know she'd gone. What he wouldn't know was where she was. Once Jack was, say ten miles away, he could smash the tag. And then go to wherever Alison had fixed up.

He'd just dumped a load, when Alison phoned. She was straight to the point.

'Can you get her to Harold Wood station car park?'

'Yes. When?'

'Soon as you can.'

She rang off and Jack went into the hotel. When he'd picked up the last load of sand, he noted that Katya was not outside. In the hotel with a punter, then. He had to get her, and be away quickly with her without being seen by Malik. Jack went up the stairs and bumped into a middle aged man, in a severe dark suit, with a young girl.

'You seen the manager?' asked the man.

'No,' said Jack. The girl was young, too young probably, a mass of eye-shadow and almost overpowering smell of hair lacquer. 'Have you tried the upstairs office?'

'He's not there,' said the man. 'This is no way to run a hotel.'

'No idea where he is,' said Jack.

'Well, if he doesn't want my money... Let's go.' He took the girl's arm.

Jack stood aside to let them go past. The girl hadn't said a word. Was she local or trafficked? No more than fifteen, he'd guess. Very short skirt, high heels, the usual uniform.

The man couldn't book a room as Malik wasn't around. That was fine as Jack didn't want to be seen with Katya as Malik would tell Potter. Why wouldn't he? Katya had room 9 on the first floor. Outside the door, he could hear huffing and puffing. He couldn't burst in. He'd have to wait until they were done.

Come on, come on, get it over with. He wished he had earplugs. This was sound porn, like a train going up hill. Soon it would blow its whistle. A sad industry, trafficked women, uncaring men, overseen by the Potters of the world.

Imagine putting a tag on a woman. Like a leash. The woman in room 6 had had one too, so Katya had said. Was she a whore too? That hadn't occurred to him. Had her pimp got to a level of extreme distrust? He'd put a tag on Norma Jean, and she'd tried to escape. From Shenfield, Hayley had said. And ended up dead in Forest Gate.

Why Forest Gate?

Perhaps she knew someone round here, and didn't want to disturb them late at night. All supposition. He must tell Fayyad that Norma Jean was wearing a tag.

This man inside was reaching his climax, not much longer. After a laboured thirty seconds, the man was done, the heavy breathing subsided to an exhausted gasp. Jack went up the hallway, not wanting to be caught outside the door as if he were the next punter in line. Katya would be out shortly. She wasn't allowed time for lying around. Once done, her punters barely had time for a quick wipe, she'd hurry them along as she had to be out on the road, hustling up the next.

A middle aged man came out, doing up his flies. On seeing Jack, he instantly stopped that action and straightened up, fingering his well trimmed moustache. In insurance perhaps, an accountant?

'Nice day,' he said to Jack.

Jack agreed. 'Cold but sunny.'

He watched him walk leisurely up the corridor and go down the stairs. The man wanted Jack to think he was a resident, and not a whore's punter. It mattered little to Jack, he didn't know the man, just wanted him done and gone.

Jack went in the room. Katya, straightening the duvet, turned in fear.

'It's only me,' he said. 'We're off. Grab your coat and flats.'

Chapter 25

'What are you doing here?' exclaimed Geela. 'It's your turn at the hotel.'

They were at home in Manor Park in the kitchen, a house they were rarely in together. Malik had just arrived.

'It's your shift!' he declared. 'I've been there all night.'

'With your whore. Which one this time? Fi, Katya or a new girl?'

She was in a paisley housecoat and had a full laundry basket. She put it down on the kitchen table.

'It's you today,' he said again. 'It's my time off. You should be there.'

'What? No whores on duty. Fi gone already?'

'See, look?' Malik had gone to the notice board. He unpinned the timetable. 'See, you today.'

She took it from him and looked it over. Then put it on the table.

'I'm not going back in while Fi is working there.'

'She's finished for today,' he said.

'I mean working there. Ever.' She flashed her hands to emphasise. 'Ever!'

'Not this again.' He was in his grey suit. A regular business man for once, complete with a regimental tie. 'We need to take bookings. Guests will leave without paying.'

'She insults me,' she said.

'You insult her.'

'I am allowed to insult her. I'm her boss.'

'No, you can't. Not if you want to keep workers.'

'I can insult a whore who is sleeping with my husband.'

'How many times do I have to tell you I am not sleeping with Fi?'

'She must be sacked. I won't have her there any longer.'

'She's a good worker. See how much she does in her four hours. Who else could do that?'

'Fi has to go.' Geela had folded her arms. She would not be moved.

'I never have to supervise her,' he insisted. 'She gets on with her work.'

'And sleeps with the owner.'

'She does not!'

'She does!'

'She does not!'

She was sitting on a chair, her back to him. Malik sat down with his back to her. Neither spoke for a minute or turned to face the other. He cleaned his nails with a file, she was folding the washing.

'You must go in,' he said.

'Not while she's working there.'

'We won't get anyone as good as her. She starts at six. Works like a slave. So reliable.'

'And sleeps with my husband.'

'She doesn't.'

'She does.'

Another silence. Malik bit his lip. She carefully folded a bath towel.

'How could we get anyone as good?' he said. 'A cook and a chambermaid rolled into one. She even takes bookings. And at minimum wage.'

'There are agencies,' said his wife. 'We can check references. I don't care if we have to take on two people. But I am not going in with Fi there.'

'She leaves at ten,' he said. 'She's not there now.'

Geela thumped the table. 'You know what I mean. With her working there. Any time!' She turned away, back to folding clothes.

Malik shook his fists. He poked his tongue out at her back. He straightened his jacket and adjusted his tie. She was forcing him into a corner. She'd regret it.

'I'll give her a month's notice,' he said.

Geela turned to him. 'See, it's all possible, Malik. I'll finish folding this washing, then I'll go in to the hotel. But I expect you to keep your word.'

Chapter 26

The woman invited Hayley in once she'd shown her police ID. Along the hallway were pots, large ones free standing, smaller ones on tables. A surprising number. Hayley took care not to brush against any.

The woman stopped outside the kitchen. She was wearing a heavy apron which she now removed and put on a hook in a row of coats and umbrellas. While she was doing so, she explained she was a potter and had a kiln in the garden shed. Her husband, a teacher, was at work.

The woman led Hayley into the kitchen. It was large and well set up with units and white goods round the side, and a table and four chairs by the wide window. She offered Hayley a coffee which she accepted. She would be here a while. With bad news to present and information to collect.

Hayley was convinced this was Norma Jean's sister. She had spent too long looking at pictures of Norma last night. The woman had a similar mouth and nose. Her hair was a different shade but that meant nothing. Her eyes were brown too. A characteristic chin, unlikely to be coincidence.

The woman gave her name as Joy and they talked casually while coffee was being made. About the house, about making a living as a potter. Joy taught it for a few hours a week and sold what she could, mostly at craft markets and online. No, she didn't have children. She would like a child but was perhaps leaving it a bit late. Maybe later in the year, but it was such a commitment.

Once the coffee was in the cafetiere, she sat down at the table opposite Hayley. Enough small talk.

'You identified the woman on the poster at Forest Gate station,' said Hayley.

'I think she's my sister. Though it's not the best of pictures. She's very pale.' Joy hesitated before saying, 'You've bad news for me?'

'I'm afraid so,' said Hayley. 'If she is your sister...' She took a deep breath. There was no way to soften it. 'The woman is dead, I'm sorry to have to tell you. She died in a local hotel without any ID. Whether she is your sister or not, I'm here to find out.' She stopped, recalling her trainer at police college telling them all to imagine it's your sister or brother. How would you like the messenger to behave?

'I am sorry to press this on you,' she said. 'It's not something I like doing, believe me. But it comes with the job.'

'I appreciate that,' said Joy, wiping an eye with the back of her hand.

'It's a family tragedy,' went on Hayley. 'For you, or if she's not your sister, for someone else. Please accept my apologies if she isn't. But we have to find out. One way or another.'

'I'd like her to be someone else,' said Joy, 'But I'm pretty sure it's Anne.'

'Anne who?'

Hayley had pen and notebook ready. She had to get full information, her boss would expect nothing less, in order to confirm the identity of the deceased or rule out this avenue.

'Anne McEwen. I haven't seen her for a couple of years,' said Joy. She sniffed, tore off a piece of kitchen roll and dabbed her eyes. 'I don't get on with her husband. He doesn't like me, I don't like him. But I did try to get in touch with Anne about a hour ago.'

'After you contacted us?'

'Yes,' said Joy. 'That photo on the poster. I thought, she looks like a corpse. But it might not be Anne. So I phoned Shenfield. That's where she lives. I don't have my sister's mobile, so I called the house phone. Fortunately, I didn't get her husband as he was out. But I spoke to the nanny. She said they hadn't seen Anne for a couple of days. They didn't know where she was.'

'Did you tell the nanny you thought she was dead?'

'No. I wasn't totally sure it was Anne even then. One hopes. So I made up some guff about wanting to talk to Anne about a family reunion.' She shrugged. 'As if.'

Joy poured coffee into mugs that she'd probably made herself. They were thick and tactile, a brown and red glaze. She took a milk jug out of the fridge, matching the cups, which she offered to Hayley.

'There is a Shenfield connection with the dead woman,' said Hayley, as she poured out milk. 'Unless she has a double living there. We'd like you to see the body, and tell us whether it is your sister or not. It's unpleasant but very necessary.'

'I can do that.'

'If we're not one hundred per cent sure, we can do DNA tests on you and the deceased, which would tell us with certainty if she is your sister or not.'

'I understand.'

'Once I've taken details,' said Hayley, 'then, if you are free, we can go off to the mortuary.'

The woman shivered. 'This is so sudden. I was thinking about Anne just the other day, wanting to get in contact again. But it's her husband, Robert. He's so controlling. She has to obey his every whim. I hate him.'

'What's his full name?'

'Robert McEwen. They have a large house on the outskirts of Shenfield. I've been there a couple of times. Years ago, when we were still talking. They have these nasty, black dogs roaming the grounds. You have to phone in advance so they can chain them up. When she was first going out with him, he was such a charmer. Good looking, rich. What a catch! Then once they'd got married, it all changed. He set her absolute limits, where she could go and where she couldn't. Early on, she wanted to drive out to Clacton-on-Sea to see our parents. He forbade it. Took her car away. As if she were a child. Total control. I'm sure she's terrified of him. I'd be. He's a monster.'

'Do you think he physically abuses her?'

'I'm sure he does. Last time I saw her, her jaw was wired up. She told me she'd fallen down the stairs but I didn't believe her. Unless he pushed her. And after that, I couldn't get in touch with her. I tried but her old mobile number was dead. I have to phone the house. I don't like speaking to the housekeeper, she's a right cow. I'm sure she lies to me. The nanny is OK. I just hope Robert doesn't answer. He just blanks me off. Tells me Anne doesn't want anything to do with her family. She's happy in Shenfield. Thank you very much, goodbye.'

'What does Robert McEwen do for a living?'

'Property development, he says. But I get the feeling some of it is pretty shady. I heard him on the phone once. The language would shock a fishwife. Telling someone to deal with someone, where to take them. It wasn't a normal business arrangement.'

'We'll see if Robert McEwen is on our records. Sounds as if he might well be. And now, if you'll let me have the details of your sister, full name, Shenfield address, date of birth and so forth. And then we'll go off to the mortuary.'

'I should be surprised about you turning up,' said Joy wearily, 'but I'm not. Not at all. Poor Anne.'

Chapter 27

Jack was leaving the car park of the hotel with Katya in the back of the van. Going slowly as if he were off to pick up something for work, his hands sweaty, neck prickly. He had put the Faraday cage over Katya's tag. If it were working, it should have shut off the tag's signal, alerting Johnny. How quick would he get on the move? It would depend what he was doing. Soon as he realised, he'd shoot over.

The back of his van wasn't made for passengers. Jack had bundled up decorating sheets, pushed back his stepladder and tool boxes, making space for Katya, assuring her it wouldn't be for long. Once out of Forest Gate, she could sit in the front.

He should be working, not leaving the hotel. It was obvious the job was half done, with mounds of sand on his workings. He had to have a reason for leaving. Personal or a small job somewhere.

He drove into the forecourt as a car was coming in. For a moment, he couldn't see the driver, the sun catching his eyes. But shielding his eyes, he saw it was Johnny. So soon! Johnny gave Jack a wave from behind the wheel, definitely him in the smart black coat and bobble hat, the thickset body.

Jack had wondered about putting the cage on straight away, but he had to as he was driving. She hadn't wanted to go into the back of the van, not trusting him. But he'd persuaded her it was too risky for her to sit in the front with him. So he'd put on the cage before driving off. He didn't trust her to do it herself in the back. He'd hoped they'd be away before Johnny spotted the signal had stopped. He must've been in the area, maybe he had other women close by, in other hotels on the Romford Road.

This was the real test for the Faraday cage. If it was working, Johnny was here because Katya's tag had gone dead. Guarding his own. Any sinner had to be caught and punished. Set an example. Stay put or you'll get the same as Katya and that builder.

Jack inched towards Johnny, holding his breath. Supposed Johnny suspected him and asked him to open his van. He could hardly refuse him. If he did refuse then Johnny would open it himself and see Katya in the back with the Faraday cage over her tag. No way to explain that.

Act normal. Machines malfunction. She'd only been cut off a few minutes. It could easily be a faulty tag. Not an escapee. He mustn't let Johnny pick up his nervousness. Behave as if this were a normal morning, and he was going off for another job. Where? Plaistow. Someone locked out of their house. Have the words ready. Just in case.

There was just room for the two vehicles to pass in the drive. Johnny stopped his car and signalled for Jack to halt, and put his head out of the car window.

'You haven't seen my woman, Jack?'

Jack attempted lightness, trying to break his rigidity.

'Who's that?' he said.

'Katya. The whore. She's one of my stable. I've lost track of her.'

'She was out front a while ago. Maybe she went for a sandwich.'

Johnny shook his head. 'She knows better than to do that. Silly cow.' His tongue lolled in his cheek. 'She could be upstairs with a punter. Where you off to?'

'Got a small job, in Plaistow. Thought I'd pop over and do it. Emergency. Someone locked out.'

'I won't keep you. These girls, hard to keep tabs on them.' He laughed. 'Malik about?'

'Might be up in his office.' He knew that he wasn't but just wanted to be away.

'I'll have a word with him. And check Katya's room. She's a busy girl. Must have that drink some time, Jack. Talk about old times. What's happened to everyone. Catch up.' He gave a thumbs up and closed his window.

Jack waved as he drove past. Slowly, don't rush. He eased into the traffic and headed off. He needed miles and miles. Johnny wasn't yet sure Katya had gone. All he knew was that she wasn't out on the road, and he was getting no signal from the tag. Could be a malfunction and she was in her room earning money.

But once he found she wasn't, then he'd know she was away. And the tag had been attacked in some way. No home range signal, no GPS ping either. He'd also know Katya couldn't do that herself; she must have had help.

Jack thought out the options that Johnny might explore. Katya might have gone to the cops and they'd disabled the tag. Though Johnny could know of her aversion to the police. So if not at the police station, where, how?

Someone must've helped her get away. Johnny was bound to come to that conclusion. He'd seen Jack leaving the hotel minutes after the signal stopped. This was awful. What had he got himself into! He had to pass Katya on as soon as he could and play dumb when Johnny came for him.

Get a move on. Jack drove down Romford Road, thinking where best to head. He couldn't go straight to Harold Wood Station, as Katya still had the tag on. It might be silenced by the Faraday Cage, but as soon as it was uncovered it would send out its signal, leading Johnny to whatever safe house Katya was taken to. And if she was caught, she'd blab. Jack's life wouldn't be worth a light.

The tag had to be permanently disabled.

Chapter 28

Fayyad didn't like autopsies. He found them unpleasant, all the innards and blood, though he'd never objected to being sent. Dead bodies were part of a detective's trade. Murders happen and it was his job to investigate them. Blood and guts were all part of the follow up. You had to know how it was done, when and who did it. Search the entrails for evidence.

Often they'd wait for the pathologist's report, but in a case like this, with so much uncertainty, an officer would attend. There were only two jobs on offer: going to see the woman's sister, unpleasant too in its way. Or here, where the stench of disinfectant and formalin soaked into his clothing. He was sensitive about his suits. Even if no one else could smell the chemicals once he'd left, he could, and would have the suit dry cleaned after each visit. He had enough in his wardrobe. Every year, he had a new suit made to measure.

The white plastic coverall and rubber boots were a poor shield for the smells. The air was acrid. He'd hate to be a pathologist, breathing it in all day, disinfecting your guts. Not a sentiment he'd ever voiced to any of the pathologists working on a body under the bright lights. To get an early opinion, you did your best to stay in their good books.

Strange job, strange people that did it. Though there were odd detectives too. But who isn't odd, one way or another? The church like silence made him reflect. Life and death. Chemicals and meat. Smelly liquid to prevent rot.

The large room was white tiled, both the walls and floor. There was a slight slope from each of the side walls, which allowed flushing into a central gutter. The pathologist,

Doctor Paul Lear, was a short black man, similarly dressed in white plastic coveralls. He was speaking in a monotone into a microphone attached to his collar as he worked.

Fayyad directed the odd question, but Dr Lear didn't welcome too many. Wait for the report, he said several times. But why come then? These professionals delighted in their power, their arcane knowledge. It wasn't as if Dr Lear didn't know why he was here. He was impatient for cause of death, believing it to be murder. Norma Jean could have died of a heart attack. If so – the end of the inquiry, move on. Or it could be foul play. Then full steam ahead. A team pulled in to find the killer.

He'd taken a call from Hayley while Lear was setting up. She'd said she was coming over with the sister, the very likely sister. The sister had talked about a Shenfield house, about the husband's possible criminal involvement and his abusive behaviour. All adding to Fayyad's conviction that Norma Jean's death was not natural. But his conviction was not enough for his boss. *Evidence, Fayyad, evidence.*

'Those bruises, Dr Lear,' he said, 'could they be connected to her death?'

'Not the prime cause. I'm picking up heart attack.'

The corpse's chest and stomach area were open. The heart and liver glistened in the low hanging, ultra bright light. The animalness of the insides nauseated Fayyad. Hardly different from a dog or an ape, the puffy intestines, the white stomach, the stickiness. Make up and clothes jettisoned, skin opened revealing pipes and goo.

There had to be a soul, he thought. More than this offal, to make us human, distinctive. Though others seeing the blood and entrails had decided there can be no soul, no God. He'd realised there must be. We are more than meat.

Fayyad wore clean clothes every day, a smart suit, showered twice, shaved morning and evening, scrubbed his fingernails. His soul deserved it. The body was a temporary shelter. The stickiness and slimy sacks, its makeshift bags and plumbing.

He wrinkled his nose, swallowed unwillingly, his throat thick with caustic. He supposed you could get used to it, but was grateful he didn't have to.

'Could it be poison?' said Fayyad.

'Possibly,' said Dr Lear. 'Some poisons will cause a heart attack. Do you suspect it?'

'I think so,' said Fayyad. 'She has some dubious family.'

'I'm sending samples up for toxic analysis,' said Dr Lear. 'Young. 35 maybe. Pregnant.'

'How long?'

'Early. Just a few months. This bruising… I'd say she'd been struck with a thick stick or something like it.'

Hayley and Joy entered the room through the swing doors. They were both togged in plastic coveralls and boots. Hayley held the other back, awaiting the call to come into the spotlights.

'Excuse me, Dr Lear,' said Fayyad. 'We, as yet, don't know the identity of the woman. But we think this lady here might be the deceased's sister.' He indicated Joy. 'Would you allow a few minutes for her to have a look and tell us whether she is or not?'

'I don't like interruptions,' said Dr Lear. 'It's not good practice.' He put a scalpel on the trolley by him. 'But in the circumstances, I will permit it.'

'Thank you very much. We are grateful,' said Fayyad, knowing he was getting a reluctant concession. 'We do need to know who she is to properly investigate.'

'I understand,' said the pathologist, already covering the corpse with a sheet to her neck. 'Relatives have to be found. Questions have to be asked.'

He wiped a streak of blood off the face of the corpse with a sponge, went round the trolley adjusting the sheet here and there.

'That will do,' he said, standing back to look at the covered body. 'Too easy to forget others' sensitivities when you've been twenty years in the job. I do need reminding sometimes.' He turned to Hayley and Joy. 'Please come over, ladies. You may see the body now.'

Hayley and Joy walked over the tiled floor to the central trolley on which the corpse lay. Only the head was revealed beneath the white plastic sheet. A pretence, thought Fayyad, that she was all there, the sheet hiding the open chest cavity with the bits removed.

'Take your time,' said Hayley to Joy.

Joy went to the head end of the trolley and stared down at the woman's face. She then went to the other side, knelt down to look closer.

'It's her,' she said. 'My sister Anne. It's her.'

'Are you absolutely sure?' said Fayyad.

'Absolutely. It's Anne. My poor, dear Anne. What did they do to you?' She began to weep. Then shook herself, wiping her eyes with a tissue. 'Excuse me, please. I wasn't sure before we came. But I am now.' She shook a fist. 'Robert did this to her, I know it.'

'We'll be going to see him,' said Fayyad.

Dr Lear said, 'Are there any identifying features? Anything on the body itself, you can recall.'

Joy thought for a few moments, then nodded. 'I'd almost forgotten,' she said. 'It was a long time ago. By the side of her right thigh is a scar, about three inches in length. She fell out of a tree when she was twelve. There was an awful lot of blood. Daddy drove her to hospital. She had fifteen stitches.'

'It's there,' said Dr Lear. 'I've noted it.'

He carefully unfolded the sheet revealing the right thigh region. On the too white skin was an old scar about three inches in length.

Chapter 29

Jack drove into a parking area in Epping Forest. It was off a main road that went through the forest. A muddy space, cleared of trees, large enough for perhaps a dozen vehicles. There was one other there; a man behind the wheel of a car was drinking tea from a thermos.

Jack had calculated that they were about twelve miles from Forest Gate. Far enough for a break and a think. He sat back in the seat, breathing slowly, stretching his arms.

'You all right back there?' he called.

'No, it's too hard, this floor,' said Katya. 'I can't get comfortable.'

'We'll sort you out in a minute,' he said.

He looked through the windscreen. The trees were winter bare and black against a blue sky, free of cloud, which reminded him of his date on the Flats with Fi in the evening. In a different world, where one had dates and laughter was allowed. In this mean world, a woman had to be passed on. One of those jobs, once begun, there can be no backing out. All or nothing. So he'd told himself on the drive up through Wanstead and Woodford. Don't get caught, or else it's curtains. Like a Cold War spy in East Berlin, given a cyanide pill in case of arrest.

'We're going to stretch our legs,' he called back to Katya.

Jack opened his door, and got out. He slid the side door open. There was Katya in her green coat, coming halfway down her thighs. She needed leggings, not those fishnets. Too late to grouse about lack of unsexy clothing. She was still in her red high heels.

She eased her way off the dirty cover sheets and onto the muddy ground.

'Put your flats on,' said Jack. 'We're going into the forest.'

'Why?' she said in alarm.

'I want to break that tag,' he said. 'I can't do it here. There's a guy in the car over there, watching us.'

She looked across. The man drinking tea was staring at them; she gave him two fingers and he looked away.

'He'll remember us,' said Jack. 'Not a good idea.'

'Christmas is not a good idea,' said Katya, 'but it still happens.'

He said nothing, trying to follow her reasoning. She obviously didn't like Christmas, but had a pessimistic acceptance. Not surprising considering her life. More like an animal than a human being.

He watched her, aware of the man in the car. She was sitting on the edge of the van taking off her heels which she replaced with flats. They were thin with little warmth in them, hardly good wear for a muddy forest, just better than high heels whose only function was to show off legs. The bulge of tag and cage was around her ankle, his improvised construction of metal and gaffer tape.

'I hope mud doesn't bother you,' he said.

'I was a farm girl,' she said. 'Mud washes off.'

Entirely sensible. He might have said that himself. She stood up, pulling the coat round herself in the chilly wind. Jack gathered a cold chisel and a hammer from the van, and slid the door shut. He led the way into the forest. There was a path, muddy as he'd expected, with puddles and boot mashed patches. The forest was always claggy in winter. Cyclists came through too, their ruts mushing up the paths even more. A few years ago, he would come to the forest with his telescope to find less polluted skies, but found it a chore and these days stuck closer to home.

Katya picked her way through, legs becoming splattered. Jack in boots and overalls was protected, mud, or plaster, his usual fare. There was no point going far in, just away from the man in the car park. And a surface to work from. Ahead, just off the path, was a fallen tree. That would do.

He led her through the brambles and sat Katya on the trunk, lifting the leg, with the tag and cage, along its length.

'I'm not feeling too good,' she said, a hand to her chest, blinking rapidly.

'What's up?'

'I need my medicine.' She coughed, making Jack wonder what it was. Was she ill?

'We'll see to that soon.'

'I need it now,' she exclaimed.

'One thing at a time,' he said. 'Let me deal with the tag and then I'll get you medicine.'

'I feel bad.'

Jack ignored her complaints. What could he offer her anyway? There were no shops around. She had no logic. Or a short term memory, forgetting already Johnny who would throttle the pair of them. Never mind a cough.

He hesitated before beginning work. While the Faraday cage was covering the tag, no signal could get out. But he was going to smash the tag. To kill it stone dead. To do so, he would have to take off the cage. But as soon as the cage came off the tag's GPS signal was freed. Johnny might well pick it up, and know where they were. But it had to be risked. The only way was to do it quickly, then get well away from here.

'I need my medicine. Johnny has my medicine.'

Some medicine, he thought. Johnny will cut the two of us to bits. Carefully, he undid the gaffer tape and took off the Faraday cage. He dropped it on to the ground. The light on the tag was flicking rapidly like an alive thing. Jack smashed at it with the hammer.

'Oh, you are hurting me!' she exclaimed.

There was a little blood seeping through her stocking.

'Sorry. I'll be more careful.'

He bashed at it with the cold chisel. Short, sharp hits to avoid her leg. The light went off, the tag was dented. He bashed on feverishly for half a minute and stopped. Was the machine dead? It looked it, but just because the light wasn't on and because the tag had dents, didn't mean it couldn't be sending out a signal.

There was only one way to be really sure.

'Stay here,' he said. 'I won't be a minute.'

'I need my medicine.'

'Soon,' he called as he ran back along the path to the car park, through the puddles and churned mud. The other car had left. It would have been easier to work out there, but how was he to know the man would go so soon? He looked at his watch and calculated how long he'd got if the tag was still working. Or even if, in those brief seconds before it was broken, it had sent a signal. 12 miles from Forest Gate. Through the traffic. It would take a minimum of 20 minutes to get here, say 25.

He slid open the van and took out his hacksaw and a couple of spare blades, slammed it shut and headed back into the forest. Katya was on the ground clutching her stomach, her legs and coat muddy.

'I need my medicine,' she wailed, rocking backwards and forwards.

'I'll get you some,' he said, 'but this has to be done first.'

He grabbed her leg, quite roughly, she was making him angry. Didn't she understand what needed to be done? He began sawing frenziedly at the tag on her ankle. Get it done. The tag was priority. It could still be singing: Here we are in Epping Forest. Come and get us, Johnny!

The metal bracelet of the tag was encased in plastic to be less abrasive against the skin. A single cut took the saw through the plastic and into the metal. Jack was at once relieved that it was not hardened steel, which could take him an hour to get through with a hacksaw. The teeth snared into the metal, making a groove. He had to hold her ankle with one hand, sawing like a surgeon on a man-o'-war while she struggled as if he were taking off her leg.

'You are hurting me!'

'I have to do this!' he yelled. 'Otherwise Johnny'll be here.'

'Johnny's got my medicine.'

'Johnny will twist your head off your neck,' he hissed, continuing to saw.

Having no doubt that he would. Once begun, this had to go through till the end. There was a killer on their tail. He could be driving this way at this very moment. Get the tag off. A vice would be so much easier than hanging on to her reluctant leg.

'Keep your leg still!' he ordered to little avail.

The blade rasped, particles flew in the damp air. And then he was through. Jack put down the saw. Thank God. He was breathing heavily with his effort. Hot.

Except the tag wouldn't come off her leg. He couldn't twist it free. Maybe with a gemmy but he couldn't use that against Katya's leg. Jack glanced at his watch. That had taken him eight minutes, if Johnny was on his way, then he still had about fifteen minutes. Time enough. Keep cool. He needed to get a whole section off to get the tag off Katya's leg.

He went back to sawing, ignoring her moaning, sitting on her leg to stop her wriggling. She was like a child. Johnny this, Johnny that, and her medicine. What would he say if some walkers came by? Sitting on the leg and sawing at the ankle of a complaining woman. Nothing at all, he'd keep on sawing. What could they do? Call the police. Fine by him. Katya might panic but then she was panicking already.

He sawed on for the next eight or so minutes, determined to get the tag free. It might be dead, if so all this effort was needless, or it might be screaming their co-ordinates. Time was ticking away. Suppose Johnny was on the way? They couldn't stay much longer.

Saw.

A speck of metal flicked into his eye. He rubbed and blinked. He should have brought his goggles out. Jack pulled down a lid and let go. It was painful. He pulled at the lid again.

'I need my medicine.'

'Shut up, shut up!'

He danced about pulling at his eyelid. There, it had gone. And he went back to sawing.

At last, he was through the metal. The tag fell away in two pieces. What to do with it? He lay it on the tree trunk, and smashed at the machine section repeatedly with the hammer, squashing it almost flat. He stopped. It had to be well and truly dead now. Had to be.

Sweating, breathing hard, he considered what to do with it. Put it back in the shield? Why bother? He flung it into the trees. If there was the slightest chance it was still going, then let Johnny come into the forest and search for it.

He grabbed Katya by the arm and pulled her after him, along the muddy path and out into the car park. Another car was there. A man and woman were looking at them. Katya was mud splattered, her coat open, revealing a short skirt and torn fishnets. Let them think what they wanted. Jack opened the front door of the van and pushed her into the passenger seat.

He ran round the other side and climbed in himself. He threw his tools behind him.

'I need my medicine,' she wailed, rocking back and forth.

'I'm going to get you some,' he said, willing to say anything to shut her up. They had to be away. 'Put your seat belt on.'

When she ignored him, he put it on for her, then his own. He looked at his watch. Twenty two minutes had passed. Almost time for Johnny to arrive if he'd picked up the signal when the cage was first taken off.

Jack set off, going the opposite way to which Johnny would be coming. If he were coming. Through forest on both sides of the road, and into the town of Epping. There, he had to slow down, the traffic busy on the high road with vehicles off the M25 and locals. Normal people walking on the pavements, with pushchairs and shopping bags. A relatively safe place, though Johnny might be at the car park by now. Then what would he do?

Jack tried to work it out. Johnny would not have a lot of options. His quarry was gone. All he could do was scout around the various roads. He might come this way, might go another. Jack had to increase the radius, decrease the chance of being found, and, at the same time, head towards Harold Wood, their rendezvous.

His phone rang. It was on the dashboard. He hesitated, but the traffic was slow through Epping. Mobile phone usage was illegal when driving. A fine and points on his license.

Dead people don't pay fines.

It was Alison.

'Where are you, Jack?'

'Had some trouble. Can't talk, I'm driving. Be there in twenty minutes.'

'We'll wait.'

He closed the call. Illegality over. Katya was doubled over and moaning. Some foreign words. There was nothing he could do for her other than get her to safety. That meant not stopping anywhere.

In a few minutes, he was out of Epping. He took side roads, figuring if Johnny was around he'd be sticking to main roads. And on, through more forest, villages, on to North Weald, down through Chipping Ongar to Brentwood. Jack of All Trades out on a job. What an identifiable van! No mistaking it, no other like it.

If Johnny suspected him, all he had to do was ask a passer-by. Jack drove his roving ad straight on, following the railway line to Harold Wood station.

He pulled in at the car park.

Alison was there with another woman by a red car. She rushed over as he opened the door.

'Where have you been?' she said.

'Round the world,' he said, unwilling to get into explanations, as he pushed the bundle of Katya out of his van.

'What's wrong with her?'

'She wants her medicine,' he said with a weary smile. 'I'm sure you can treat her.'

Alison led Katya away, soothing her. 'You're safe with us. Don't worry. We'll look after you.'

Until Jack could hear them no more. Gone, out of his life. Liberated and alone. He was shivering, but it wasn't cold affecting him. He'd make a lousy soldier. Rubbing at his thighs and hips, easing his breathing, he watched as Katya was put into the back seat of the car. Their responsibility. He was free of her. Alison and the woman were talking to her over the seat. Nothing to do with him any longer.

Jack climbed into his van and set off back.

Chapter 30

Fayyad and Hayley parked a little way up from the wide, wrought iron gates. As they alighted two large black dogs raced down the drive, snapping and barking. At the fence, their snouts poking through the railings, slobbery teeth glinting in the sunlight, they continued their fierce warning.

'Nice to be welcomed,' said Hayley, keeping her distance from the fence.

The dogs' snouts followed them, a punctuated barking, not quite in sync. Fayyad and Hayley walked to the gate. The dogs poked their heads between the ironwork, frantic to be through and at them. On either side of the gates were red brick pillars with white pyramidal tops, like marquees at a fair. Inset into the pillar was an intercom. Fayyad pressed the button, watching the dogs snapping and prancing, as close as they could get.

'Who is it?' came a voice.

'Detective Sergeant Kamani and Detective Constable Amis,' he yelled into the speaker above the barking.

'Wait.' A single word from a female, as if to say more would reveal too much.

Fayyad stepped back a couple of yards to join Hayley, the dogs in fury by the gate, at the couple who would not leave their territory.

'What would they do to someone who climbed over?' mused Fayyad.

'Tear him to bits,' said Hayley.

'What would we do if he refuses to talk to us?' he said.

'Write him a letter,' said Hayley. 'I'm not going in unless I'm in a tank.'

The dogs were feverish, non-stop brawn. Presumably they wound each other up. One barking because the other was. How did you breed such killers? All muscle, teeth and hatred. You couldn't call them evil, thought Fayyad, because they knew nothing else. No doubt, they were well fed. Unthinking brutes. Not unlike some criminals he'd come across.

They waited, nothing seemed to be happening. The dogs barked on. It seemed they would forever, till the trespassers left their territory. The house was set back about fifty metres from the gate. A wide driveway expanded to a semi circle in front of the flat roofed house. It had two stories, modern, much of it glass, long purple drapes on both floors.

On the ground floor, through the window, a man was holding the curtain aside and watching them.

Fayyad went to the intercom and pressed again.

'Wait,' said the female voice.

'We have waited,' said Fayyad.

'Wait some more.'

Fayyad smiled at the added words. He didn't continue with the conversation, suspecting he'd get no more information, just the repeated words, as if she were an automaton programmed with a few stock phrases. Or an underling, much the same thing in the circumstances, relaying what she'd been told she must say.

The dogs had quietened. Fayyad noted that if they stood stock still, the dogs simply watched, daring them.

'Shall I phone them?' said Hayley. 'This is a bit of a liberty. I said we were coming.'

'Look!' Fayyad pointed.

The front door had opened, a burly man in a black suit, like an undertaker, came out. His hair was short and receding, his face very red. He was carrying two heavy chains, and in no hurry, as he made his way down the drive. Visitors had to wait. It put them in their place.

'Sit!' croaked the man as he neared the dogs.

They obeyed instantly, sitting like obedient stone. He snapped the chains onto their collars.

'Wait,' he said to Fayyad and Hayley. And led the dogs down the drive and round the side of the house.

'What a waste of time,' said Hayley.

'He doesn't welcome visitors.'

'I wouldn't come twice.'

The man had gone round the side of the house. They waited, wondering what would happen next. The man who had been watching through the curtain was no longer. All quiet. Something had to happen. A woman and a man had told them to wait. The dogs had gone.

The gates slowly opened.

'Let's drive in,' said Fayyad. 'In case they let the dogs out.'

'She lived here, Norma Jean. Anne, I mean,' reflected Hayley. 'No wonder she wanted to escape.'

'Like Dracula's Castle,' said Fayyad, 'but less welcoming.'

They went back to the car and Hayley drove slowly through the gates which closed behind them. She headed to the front of the house. The high front door had opened and a woman was standing there.

The door was a sheet of frosted glass with an engraving of Pan merrily blowing his pipes. The woman was in black like the man who had taken the dogs away. She wore a mid-length pleated skirt and a black short sleeved blouse. She was middle-aged, her hair black as her clothing. She wore no make up.

'Come this way, please.'

Fayyad and Hayley followed her into the house into a large atrium, high and wide. The floor was gleaming, white tiles. Around the side were Greek statues of young men and girls, about half size, raised from the ground on white plinths. In the centre was a pool with a fountain in the centre gushing from the mouth of a boy clutching a fat fish.

Lighting aimed at the fountain, dazzled them in its sparkle. Beyond was a wide curved staircase.

The woman took them to a side room with a frosted glass double-door. She opened one of them.

'Please go in,' she said. 'You are expected.'

She left them and they entered a room the size of a hall. A chandelier with dangling glass and a circle of small lights hung from an ornate ceiling with a palaeolithic scene of mammoths, wild cattle and sabre-tooth cats. It was bewildering, like a museum where they had left the classical hall to go back to the old stone age. The carpet was thick and white, almost like a fur coat. Fayyad was tempted to take off his shoes, loath to sully it. There was a cream semi-circle of sofa, with room for ten, with three matching armchairs, facing a huge fire, the flames crackling and darting into the room. Too huge, it wasn't safe even in a room this size. Or hot.

'A hologram,' said a voice from the far end of the room. 'Effective, ain't it?'

A London accent. A working class boy who'd gone up in the world. He came towards them. He was short and dressed in white. The symbolism obvious to Fayyad. Underlings in black, the boss in white. White suit, white shirt, white tie, his shoes too were white. Fayyad wondered whether he had other colours in his wardrobe. Or whether he'd changed especially for their visit. They were, after all, only cops, hardly worth any fuss.

The man's hair was short, almost shaven. He had a stubby nose, perfect teeth, and large ears, almost cabbage like. Fayyad recognised him and wondered whether he'd been recognised in turn.

'Mr McEwen?' he said.

'That's me.' He smiled. 'Sorry about the wait. But we had some trouble a few months back.'

'Annoying visitors?' said Fayyad.

The man shrugged. 'A little trouble, but we dealt with them. Once bitten, you might say. Now we inspect visitors more closely. There's a telescope on the roof.'

'I didn't see it,' said Fayyad.

'You wouldn't,' said the man. He was peering closely at Fayyad. 'I think I know you.' He snapped his fingers. 'Cumberland school.'

Fayyad smiled. 'Small world.'

'What's your name? Don't tell me. Cricket. Ace batsman. Begins with F…Fayyad!' he yelled in triumph and pumped Fayyad's hand vigorously. 'Fancy you being a copper. What's your full moniker?'

'Detective Sergeant Fayyad Kamani. And this is my colleague, Detective Constable Hayley Amis.'

'Pleased to meet you both.' He shook Hayley's hand. 'This is a surprise. I knew the law was coming but never expected an old pal. There's a turn up for the books. You a copper, Fayyad. Well, well.' He looked Fayyad up and down. 'Smart suit. You always were well turned out.'

'No one noticed at Cumberland.'

'I did. These things matter. Why be a slob all your life? But please, sit down. What will you think of me?' He ushered them to the sofa. There were two frosted glass-topped coffee tables in front with engraved mammoths and rhinos. McEwen took an armchair. 'Now what can I get you? A drink. The odd one, I'm sure, is alright.'

'Coffee,' said Fayyad.

'Me too,' said Hayley.

There was a remote on the arm, McEwen picked it up. 'Felicity, three coffees. And bring some pastries for my guests, there's a love.'

'You've done well for yourself, Noddy.'

The man laughed. 'No one's called me that in twenty years.' He leaned forward. 'And I'd rather you didn't. Not here leastways. It's Robert. No, make it Bob. We don't need any of that Mr McEwen stuff.' Then he recalled the comment. 'Yeh, haven't done badly, have I?' gesturing around. 'Not for a kid from Plaistow.'

'What's the secret?'

'No secret, Fayyad. Property. Once you've made the first million, the rest is a doddle. Buy more. But remember, always do a survey first. And buy. In a rising market, how can you go wrong? Any idiot can do it. Increasing population, more kids coming all the time. It's obvious. Prices may go down for a bit, but then up they shoot. How can they not? Supply and demand. There's only so much land to go round.' He was enjoying giving his economics lesson, beaming at the class of two. But then recalled, the levity wasn't quite right. His face set sternly. 'But you haven't come out to Shenfield to learn business, have you, mate?'

'I'm sure you've a lot to teach, Bob. But no. Hayley told your housekeeper over the phone.'

'I gave her brief details,' said Hayley. 'I couldn't get through to you, Mr McEwen. She wouldn't put me through.'

'Yeh, well. That's her job.' He held a hand up. 'I know where we're at. Anne's dead. And that's why you're here. Not to look up an old mate.'

'She was found dead in a Forest Gate hotel two days ago,' said Fayyad. 'No ID, which is why we've taken this long getting to you. But we've been able to contact her sister and she gave a positive identification of the body.'

'Never got on with Joy,' said McEwen. 'Her and her teacher husband. I'm not arty enough for 'em.'

'I think you've some appreciation...' began Fayyad, gesturing around.

'Nah. It's all show. The architect and designer showed me some pictures. And I said this, that, and those. Art is for posers. And you might say I'm a bit of a poser. But then what's money for? Mind you, I don't like it when someone comes here and turns up their nose. Like Joy did. Guests shouldn't do that.'

'No, they shouldn't,' said Fayyad, keen to be agreeable. 'When did you first know your wife had gone?'

'She left without telling me,' said McEwen with a shrug. 'Didn't know she was gone till the morning.'

'She hasn't got a car?'

'Doesn't need one.'

'So she must've walked to the station.'

'I expect so.'

'Quite a way.'

He shrugged. 'I don't know. I never go by train.' He leaned forward, pressing his hands together. 'Is there some reason why the Forest Gate police had to come out here in person? It's quite a long way. The local law could've given me the news.'

The door opened and the housekeeper entered with a trolley. She pushed it across the prairie of carpet and halted by the sofa. She was about to begin pouring when McEwen said:

'Leave it to us, Felicity. We've got things to discuss.'

She bowed slightly. 'Yes, Mr McEwen.' And turned about.

It was only once she'd left the room that conversation recommenced. Hayley went to the trolley and poured out the coffee, into delicate cups patterned with Chinese women in dresses to their ankles and ornate hairdos.

'Anne is dead,' said McEwen. 'I get that. Poor woman. Black for me, dear.' He turned back to Fayyad. 'But why are you here?'

'We're not sure about the cause of death,' said Fayyad. 'Could be heart attack or could be...' He hesitated.

McEwen jumped in. 'Murder? Are you suggesting she might have been bumped off?'

'Possibly. There are suspicious circumstances.'

'Like what?'

'I'm not at leave to say, if you don't mind.'

'I do mind. She's my wife, Fayyad. You think she's been murdered, so I've a right to know what you know.'

'All I'm at liberty to say at the moment is that she was found on Monday morning in a hotel in Forest Gate. Dead.'

'You come all this way to tell me that?'

He'd stood up, his face had reddened, his body ready to fight. Fayyad recalled Noddy McEwen at school, a tempestuous bully.

'I am sorry for your loss, Bob. I know it's hard...'

'Tell me what you know or get out.'

'Bob...'

'Don't Bob me. You want to hear from me, you tell me what I ask or you leave my house. No ifs no buts. Give me the low down.'

'I can't tell you any more. Her death is under investigation.'

'Then bugger off. I won't talk to the law without a lawyer. How dare you come here, a petty detective sergeant with a bean pole of an assistant. I want to speak to your boss. You intrude on my household, abuse my hospitality. How dare you! Get out!'

Fayyad rose. He looked to Hayley. She nodded.

'I'm sorry for your loss...'

'Leave my premises or I'll set the dogs on you.'

The message was unambiguous. Hayley and Fayyad headed for the door.

'Felicity,' exclaimed McEwen into the house-phone, 'the cops are leaving. Right now. See they don't come back.'

Chapter 31

Jack had returned to work. He must go on as if nothing had happened. His story was that he had been away for two hours on a small job and was now back on his main one. Making up for lost time, Betelgeuse was going to and fro, picking up sand and dumping it in place. Automatic work, as he could work the controls without thinking, but cold work. He hadn't eaten today, not since Fi's bacon sandwich, hours ago. And a kiss.

Which was blown away by Katya. A mad run out to Epping Forest to break her electronic tag, miles away from the hotel. Work, pretend there was no interruption. Fi had kissed him, they'd arranged a date on the Flats. Then he'd gone back to work, as if nothing had intervened. He had ferried sand all day long, no one came to ask for help. No one scared him out of his wits, driving in as he was driving out with a woman in the back of the van.

A useless pretence. It had happened. He had helped Katya escape, even though she'd been remarkably ungrateful. He wondered how Alison and the woman were getting along with her. Had they found some medicine for her? Was she saying thank you to any one of those who had gone out of their way to assist her?

Work. In spite of the cold. In spite of hunger. Carry on until the excitement fades.

He was shivering when Johnny Potter drove in. Jack was out the back dumping a load. Johnny drove through the arch and parked his car next to Jack's van. Did he ever take off that bobble hat? Jack had been expecting him. Knew he would come. And that he had to face him. Sooner or later. Get it done with.

Johnny came over and shouted over the noise of the digger. 'Have you seen Katya?'

'I haven't.'

Jack turned off the digger and rose from the seat. He lay his cold hands on the hot engine, rubbing in the heat.

'Oh, I'm frozen. So cold on that machine.'

'Did you do that job in Plaistow?'

Jack had to think for a second. What in Plaistow? His brain was frozen too. Ah yes, the tale he'd told earlier. Be consistent with your lies.

'Yes,' he said. 'Easy enough job. A door jammed.'

'I was hoping the bitch would be back,' said Johnny. 'I've been all over looking for her. Even up Epping Forest.'

'Why Epping Forest?'

'Heard it on the grapevine.' He smiled, tapping his temple with his forefinger.

'Why would she go there?' said Jack, ever helpful.

'That's what I thought. Strange place to go this time of year. Katya's not the sort of girl to hug trees. She likes city streets. Been with me three years. And then to go off like that. Without a word. Epping Forest?'

'No accounting,' said Jack, hoping Johnny would leave him be.

'Someone might've got her.' He shook his head. 'That's my worry. She could be in trouble. Stupid bitch, leaving without telling me. I've five girls up and down this strip. It's my job to keep 'em safe. Who knows what trouble she's in?'

Jack wondered whether he had all his girls tagged. Or whether Katya was an experiment.

'I'll keep looking,' said Johnny. 'I just want her to be safe. I got a responsibility to all my girls. But enough for today. I'm up Shenfield tonight. A poker game with an old pal.' He slapped Jack on the back. 'Course, you know him! Remember Bob McEwen from school?'

'You mean Noddy McEwen?'

Johnny laughed. 'Don't ever let him hear you say that! He's got some temper.'

'Always had.'

'If you're not doing anything, you could come along. I'll vouch for you. He's got this amazing house. Like a palace. You wouldn't believe it, how much he's made. I thought I was doing well, but he makes me seem like a beggar. Fancy a game of poker?'

'Got a date,' he said, relieved to have his get-out. He'd never liked Noddy. He'd been a bully at school, carried a knife even in those days. Rumour was he'd used it too. Not that Jack could afford poker with Tosser and Noddy. They wouldn't be playing for pennies. And the booze would flow like a mountain stream. The last place he wanted to go.

'Some other time then,' said Johnny. 'See you, mate.'

He gave a flick of a wave and strolled towards his car, that cocky confidence as if he owned the world. Jack watched him as he came to Jack's van. The side door was open. Jack had been ventilating it, getting rid of Katya's smell. Cheap perfume and body odours. Johnny looked in, had he smelt her? It must have wafted away by now. He'd had it open since he'd been back. Johnny bent forward, head deep into the van, legs barely on the ground. What was he up to? Smelling something. He hoped not. What would he say to Johnny about it?

Johnny came out of the back, and swung round with a pair of high-heeled, red shoes in one hand. Jack's stomach twisted in dread as Johnny, holding the shoes up like a trophy, marched back to Jack. His face fierce and determined, demanding an explanation where there wasn't one. Or not one that would save him.

Jack had completely forgotten about the shoes when he'd handed Katya over at Harold Wood. Only too eager to pass her on. He had to come up with something or Johnny would kill him.

'Where the hell did these come from?' He was swinging them about his head like a slingshot as if he might let fly.

'I found them in the bin,' said Jack. 'That one.' He pointed to a wheelie bin. 'I threw some rubbish in and saw them. I was going to tell you about them.'

'But you didn't.'

'I was cold. I forgot.'

'What were you going to do with the shoes?'

'Give them to my date tonight.'

'You like kinky shoes?'

'Yeh.'

Johnny stared at him until Jack couldn't take it, and looked away. Had he been believed? It was feeble. But the best he could manage on the spot.

Johnny poked him in the chest. 'You know what an electronic tag is, Jack?'

'Something they put on a guy's ankle instead of sending him to prison.'

'That's it. You know how to silence one?'

'Never thought about it.'

'Katya had one on her ankle. And it cut off like a switch when she was here this morning. Somewhere around the hotel. And then came on for a few seconds in Epping Forest. How would you account for that?'

'I can't. Unless some electrician helped her.'

'What do you know about electrics?'

'How to change a light bulb.'

Johnny stared at him, as if trying to see into his head, to read his fear. Jack had little doubt what Johnny would do if he believed Jack had crossed him.

Johnny threw up his hands. 'You're just a thicko builder. Jack of All Trades. Sand and cement is your measure. It's why you're grubbing away at jobs like this. No ambition, that's your trouble. Bobby McEwen wouldn't use you for a rag to clean out his swimming pool.' He swung the shoes. 'I'll keep these.'

And he headed off to his car.

Chapter 32

Jack was at home after work. He'd transported all the sand, from bales to site, but hadn't raked it level. He had worked hard this afternoon, but was behind schedule. Inevitable with his break with Katya and the period when the site had been part of the crime scene.

Could be worse. Pretend it had rained, and hours lost, waiting for it to stop. That would have been less hazardous than running around with Katya. Having Johnny Potter nosing about.

Potter worked through fear. That's how he kept his women in place. Terrified them. So sure of himself that he'd told Jack what he was doing. Fear worked. Made his money, kept him out of jail. But to maintain fear, it had to be crystal clear what he'd do if you transgressed. Jack didn't give a hoot that Johnny thought him a fool. Fine. The more fool the better. If only Johnny would keep on believing it. But would he, once he connected the red shoes to Jack leaving in the morning just after Katya's tag had cut out?

Johnny must be homing in, and heaven help Jack then. He recalled at school, Johnny had brought in a mouse. A group of them had watched while he cut off its legs with a razor blade and left it struggling in the dust. One of the boys, Sam, had put the animal out of its misery. And Johnny had broken Sam's nose.

An example to them all.

Should he go to the cops? Except he had no faith the police could protect him. If Johnny decided Jack was involved in Katya's escape then he didn't need to do the dirty work himself. He was sure to have an eager apprentice, keen to do him a favour.

Jack considered phoning Alison to find out about Katya. Except the less he knew the better. For Katya and for him. For Alison too. Katya was not his concern any longer. He had got her away, that was more than could be expected of him. Stupid of him. Johnny was right; he was a fool. He should have dropped her off at a police station, no matter how much Katya squawked.

He was a useless vigilante.

Maybe he should go to that poker game in Shenfield. Lose all his money and win Noddy and Johnny's sympathy. How could Johnny kill him then? The big loser. But the thought of driving up with Johnny, making small talk all the way from Forest Gate to Shenfield. Johnny going on about Katya, what he'd do when he got her again. Wondering how much coincidence was allowable. Jack would flatter him, say what a smart car he had, how his body was in great shape.

Johnny would see through it. Surely? As for the poker game... They'd be betting in twenties and fifties. That would barely see him through a single round. He'd be borrowing from game two, the high rollers annoyed. Who brought this penniless punk?

Anyway, he had a date with Fi. And that was affordable. He wouldn't need to sell his soul. But he needed to be in a better state than this.

His phone rang as he was dressing. It was Mia.

'Hello, Dad.'

'Hello, Mia. How's it going?'

'I'm in this string quartet,' she said. 'You know? Two violins, a viola and a cello.'

'You said that was a fate worse than death.'

'When did I say that?'

'Maybe I misheard.'

'You did. It's great. We've got this piece to play on Thursday evening. A bit from Carmen. It's really zippy. Hard though, but it races along. You are coming?'

'Wouldn't miss it for anything.'

'You always say that.'

He had missed a few events. It had to be admitted. He wasn't comfortable in schools, secondary especially. They reminded him of his Cumberland days. He never did much work there; the teachers gave him a hard time; so he'd done even less, and they gave him a harder time. At Mia's school events, as a parent, he felt the people around were stuffed with qualifications, the walls berating him for having the gall to come in. And as for teachers... He'd actually married one. Was it guilt or was it fear? Was it the vain hope she'd educate him?

'I'll be there,' he insisted.

'Promise?'

'I promise.' Maybe he'd invite Fi. That's if tonight went all right. 'I'll be there. Don't worry.'

'Wear a suit.'

'OK.' She was adding stress. A suit? She might as well have said a ball and chain. Well, he could always ignore that instruction. Suits were for bankers.

'We had the afternoon off to practise,' she said. 'The quartet. We had the music room all to ourselves, the four of us. We had a laugh. But a good practice. I've got this cello solo, the others stop and I have to zip through like a lighted taper. If I can carry it off... We're going to be excellent. And we want to carry on. Not just for the concert, but being a quartet, not just a scratch group for a school concert.'

'Sounds great.'

'Of course we'll have to come up with a repertoire. Miss Pamuk said she'd show us some pieces. It's so exciting.'

'Wouldn't you rather be in a rock band?'

'There's more than one sort of music, Dad.'

He was suitably chastised.

'Well, I'm looking forward to Thursday. Break a leg.'

'That's what actors say. Not musicians.'

'Break a string then.'

'That would be disaster!'

'Not as bad as a broken leg would be.'

'I could play with a broken leg, but not with a broken string,' she said. 'This conversation is getting silly. See you Thursday. I've booked you and Mum seats.'

So no Fi, then. Sitting next to Alison. Well, that was bearable. They wouldn't have to talk much, listen to the music, wait for Mia to come on. He would not mention Katya and hoped Alison wouldn't either.

'You'll be great,' he said. 'Knock 'em dead.'

'Bye.'

She rang off. He caught himself smiling. The phone call had picked him up. There was another world, where people played cellos and weren't out to get you. He must have a bite to eat before he went out.

PART FOUR:
BETELGEUSE OR BUST

Chapter 33

Jack had packed the telescope in the van, cosseting it in a blanket as if it were a baby. The mount lay alongside and the binoculars in a plastic bucket. All set. It was icy cold, car roofs laced with frost. He adjusted his scarf and pulled his collar round. He was wearing two pairs of socks and thick gloves. While he was viewing, he'd switch to fingerless gloves as he couldn't manage the telescope dials with normal gloves.

He still hadn't done the estimate for Malik, for dividing room 6. Come to that, he hadn't had the chance to look at the room again as Fayyad had asked him to. Katya had intervened, taken three hours out of his life with Faraday cages and trips to Epping. He hadn't spoken to Fayyad since late last night; the investigation must have moved on. The police would now know whether Norma Jean was from Shenfield or not. If so, was she running away? Seemed the most likely explanation. No ID, no money. Though that could've been stolen from her, if she was murdered. Her killer not wanting her identified.

He'd tell Malik that he needed to check his measurements for the estimate. But was there any point really? He recalled Malik, Fi and himself outside the room, the key stuck in the lock from the inside. So how had the murderer left? If it wasn't a heart attack.

Katya said that she'd been in the room, in a sex party with Johnny and Malik. She'd said Norma Jean had been wearing a tag. That was something Fayyad wouldn't know as she didn't have it on in the morning when she was found.

Who took it off?

It hit him. Johnny. The one that went on Katya may well have been the one taken off Norma Jean's ankle. Though it didn't have to be, he conceded. Johnny might just have seen it on Norma and thought – what a good idea!

Enough police work. They weren't paying him.

Did he have everything? Telescope and mount, binoculars, a thermos and a folding chair. He was used to the cold, working out in all weathers. And once absorbed in the night sky, he could watch till numbness set in. But he couldn't expect that of Fi. Hence the chair and thermos. She could sit down and warm up with the coffee, wrapped in the telescope blanket.

Was this going to work? He was unsure. It was marrow bone chilly tonight. Easily the coldest night of winter. It was one thing for him to freeze, out there with his telescope, he was used to it, quite another starting a relationship that way. A few had been lost with his persistence. There was that woman, what was her name? who'd turned up in high heels. He tried to cancel when he saw how badly she was dressed, but she wasn't allowing it. So they'd driven out to Epping Forest, where he'd loaded the telescope on to the wheel-barrow while she followed him along the muddy track. Suddenly there was a scream. She'd lost a shoe in a puddle. He'd managed to fish it out, black and muddy. She was shivering, standing on one leg like a wading bird. They'd given up then and there. He'd wheelbarrowed her to where he'd parked the van. She didn't say a word all the way back to Forest Gate. What was her name?

At least, he'd got a story out of it. Told it a few times since. Did she have her own tale to tell? Probably. About a stupid builder who'd forced her to go to Epping Forest on the coldest night of the century. Mud up to her knees. Piling on the privations. That's how you told a story.

Marlene. That was her name.

He turned on the van engine as his phone rang.

'I'm so sorry, Jack,' said Fi. 'My mother's ill. It's the cold weather. I've got to go over to Eltham. She may have to go to hospital.'

'I'm sorry about that,' said Jack, realising the date was off, disappointed but relieved. He'd invite her out for a meal or the cinema on another day, not this cold weather stuff. He shouldn't inflict his hobby on his dates. If he wanted dates.

'I was so looking forward to it,' she said. 'I was all dressed up for the Arctic: scarf, hat and welly boots, ready for a blizzard when her neighbour phoned. It's Mum's asthma. This weather makes it worse. So sorry, Jack. Oops, that's my doorbell! Be my taxi. We'll fix something else up. Promise. See you in the morning.'

'It's OK, Fi. You go to your mum. See you tomorrow.'

He sat back, reflecting on the call. He'd wanted to see her, but was relieved that she'd pulled out. And he wondered whether her mother was ill. Convenient. Maybe for both of them. The night at the theatre had been a disaster. Why add to it by inviting her to a cold night on the Flats?

Of course, she might've enjoyed it. You never know. He didn't know her well enough. Which is why it was a good thing tonight hadn't happened. She might be up for it, she might hate it.

Then again, Fi was tough. She was at the hotel at six every morning and worked hard till ten, and then was off to rehearsals. She was no delicate flower, so it might well have been a good evening.

He drove off.

Or she might have pretended. '*Wonderful, darling*'. And turned down any future offer.

Jack was the only person on Wanstead Flats that night. The temperature was well below zero, the coldest for ten years. He wheelbarrowed the telescope to the centre of the Flats, as far from street lights and houses as he could be. He set up the telescope, then the folding chair with the blanket and thermos.

And looked at the stars.

The Pleiades were a gift for his binoculars. A crown of glowing stars that would be lost in the extra power of the telescope. According to mythology they were the daughters of Atlas, though how he'd found time to have daughters while holding up the World... Perhaps he'd rested on the moon. Or, being Atlas, didn't need to.

Then on to Orion, the constellation of Winter. The big rectangle with the red giant, Betelgeuse, in one corner. The namesake of his digger. A hundred thousand times larger than the sun. He sort of remembered that. Could it be true? Astronomy figures were easy to muddle. He must check it on Google. He recalled that if it were to replace the sun, it would engulf Mercury, Venus, Earth and be out beyond Mars.

What a name for the little digger!

The three stars of Orion's belt were bold and bright. Below them was his dagger. That's what Jack was going for, the second star in the dagger. Orion's nebula. Red and fuzzy, dotted with stars, against the blackness of outer space. One of the seedbeds of the universe, where new stars are made out of the debris of the old.

We are stardust, we are golden.

By the time he'd got to the sliver of moon, Jack was frozen, stomping his feet, thermos empty. He was grateful that Fi hadn't come. Nothing spoilt. It didn't matter whether her mother was ill or not. Just that she wasn't here with ice cold feet and blue lips.

Too numb to turn the dials on the telescope, he gave up. It was a mean trick to make the best nights of viewing the coldest. Packing up was painful. He blew uselessly into his fingers and slapped his chest. Pushing the wheelbarrow back across the Flats, crunching the frost, he felt like Captain Scott on his doomed expedition to the South Pole.

On the way back home, he bought a pizza.

Chapter 34

Jack arrived at the hotel in the morning. He had decided to begin his working day with a visit to room 6 as he'd promised Fayyad. Get that over and done with. He took his step ladder out of the van, and carried it through the lounge where a few guests were seated at the tables awaiting breakfast. Sounds of frying and music were coming from the kitchen. He wouldn't interrupt Fi who would be at full speed, but headed upstairs to do his recce of the walls and ceiling of room 6 for any hidden doors or recesses.

At the bottom of the stairs, he had to halt, as a girl he recalled from the day before was clomping down in high heels and short skirt, her make-up smudged. She gave him a half smile of recognition. Behind her was a portly, almost bald man in a rumpled grey suit.

'Breakfast is nearly ready,' said Jack.

'I could eat for a squadron,' said the man with a wink.

Jack let them go, wondering the age of the girl. What about the girl's parents, the Council, someone must be responsible. Malik didn't care, but someone should.

He headed up the stairs, the ladder over his shoulder. He had to manoeuvre it into the corridor, where he rested the ladder against the wall. Water was running somewhere, a Joni Mitchell song playing. He'd been thinking of her last night on the Flats. *We are stardust.*

Jack turned the handle of room 6 and pushed. The room was locked.

Not again.

'Who's that?' called a male voice. To Jack's relief. Someone alive inside.

'My mistake,' he called back.

'Well, leave us be, we need to sleep,' said the resident grumpily.

'Sorry.'

He stepped back; he should've checked whether the room was occupied. Well, he knew now. And they were going to sleep on for an hour or two. So that was the first job of the morning blown. No point taking the ladder back downstairs. It was OK where it was, though he made sure it was secure and wouldn't fall on anyone. He'd come back later to investigate the room.

Going through the lounge, there were half a dozen at the tables, chatting with half an eye on the kitchen. Bacon and egg smells wafted, making him too aware of his light breakfast. Just toast and tea before going out, hoping for a fill up on the remnants when Fi had fed this lot.

Outside, he set to raking the sand, the last layer before the cement was laid on top. A good firm bed was necessary, too little foundation material and the cement would crack and sink under the weight of vehicles. And Malik could sue him. Did Malik do that sort of thing? That would be a pain.

Do a good job.

Still chilly, his breath smoking in the air, Jack was relieved not to be on the digger. He'd be a block of ice, motionless on the machine. Much colder than yesterday. Raking, though, was beginning to warm him. He levelled the heaps, getting them flat by eye, and then checking with his spirit level and a long plank.

Once the sand was levelled, he went over it with Betelgeuse to compact it, back and forth a few times. He was done when the two smokers came out for their pre-work puff. He wondered how long they were staying. Clem and what's his name. Had he been told? Did he need to know?

Jack remembered the names of clients, had to, girlfriends, their names repeated in phone calls and fantasies, while others floated in a sort of wreckage that might reveal a name, or might not.

'Cement next?' said Clem, his legs stretched out comfortably, while his mate rolled the morning joint.

'I have to put forms in,' said Jack. And seeing his puzzlement, added, 'Wooden planks on the outside to hold in the cement. They come out when the cement is firm enough.'

'More to this than one would imagine,' said Clem. 'I can see why it's Jack of All Trades.'

Jack brought over the planks for the forms from his van and set his bench up as he'd need to saw them to size. He was marking up the planks when Fi came out with three coffees. She gave him a bright smile, making him feel still a favoured one.

'Good morning,' he said taking a coffee from her. 'I hope your mother was OK.'

'She's fine now,' she said. 'Though I was at the hospital till ten. It cost me a fortune in taxis. I never take them for myself. Walk or bus. Still, had to be done.' Then recalling. 'Did you go on Wanstead Flats?'

'I did. A great night. Though it was chilly. Maybe just as well you didn't come. Brilliant for stars, cold on the feet.'

'All quiet in the kitchen this morning,' said Clem pointedly.

Fi turned to him. 'You sound disappointed, Clem.'

'Gives us something to talk about.' He laughed as the joint came his way. 'Though Room 6 was on the bounce last night.'

'I bet room 5 was too.' She winked at them, then turned to Jack. 'Breakfast?'

'Please.'

'Got to feed the workers,' she said to the two smokers, as she and Jack went inside.

The lounge was empty, the tables half cleared. In the kitchen, Jack was surprised to see a breakfast on the table. Two eggs, beans, bacon, sausages and toast.

'Get started,' she said quietly. 'I'm only supposed to give you leftovers. Geela would go mad, but then she always goes mad whenever she sees me. Any excuse. Malik might say a word too, but in quiet.' She imitated him. 'You're feeding the builder all the profits, Fi. You think I own a bank? I wish, I wish.'

Jack laughed at the take off, and began demolishing breakfast as Fi cleaned the kitchen.

'Does Geela always sleep in room 6 when she's here?' he asked.

'Usually. But not since the woman was found. I expect she will soon enough. She won't sleep in the office, even though Malik says she's using up a paying bed. Like last night, she stayed in a guest room up top. She's gone now. Thank goodness. Malik came in about eight, out she went. Though she took my first breakfast. I didn't say a word. She said a few, but I let her run on.' She was filling the dish-washer. 'I'm good at that. Comes of being mixed race. You get it from both sides. The whites because you're black, the blacks because you're not black enough and you've got a white mother.'

'I thought that was all done with these days. Meghan Markle marrying a prince.'

He was wiping egg and beans with toast, sipping coffee.

'Don't you believe it. Everyone's racist. Scratch anyone just a little. Some shade of colour, a foreign accent – and they're counting the spoons. It used to knock me flat when I was a kid. Playground stuff. I talk back now. I simply won't take it.'

'Where's your dad from?'

'Jamaica. We left when I was four. Mum brought me and my brother up in Canning Town. He was a builder. Still might be for all I know. I haven't seen him in ten years. Married again, living Tottenham way, last I heard. Another family. I don't care. He had no interest in us; why should I honour my father?'

'You have to earn it,' he said, thinking of Mia, and the concert coming up. She'd been eight when he'd left. Or rather, when Alison had thrown him out.

She turned to him, cloth in hand from wiping the tops. 'We have to make up for last night's non event.'

'I thought a movie,' he said. 'Stratford Picturehouse. Four screens. Warm inside,' he added between mouthfuls of sausage.

'Good idea. I haven't been to the flicks for a while. Let's check what's on. You're making short work of that.'

'You said eat up.'

'I'm not complaining. A good breakfast was the least I could offer. Must get up to the rooms. Put your plate in the dishwasher and set it going, if you will.'

She gave him a kiss on the cheek and was away. The swiftly moving Fi bird.

Jack finished his meal, and washed it down with coffee. He put the crockery and utensils in the dishwasher. He pressed 'Start' and left as water splashed in. Outside it had warmed a little. Forms to put in. But first, tidy the remnants of sand at the entrance before someone complained. He'd noted it when he'd driven in this morning.

He drove Betelgeuse out. The digger had a small bulldozer front, used for pushing earth or sand around. Under the arch he went, and saw her as he was coming through. There, out on the pavement, short leather skirt, and red high heels.

Katya.

She'd come back! All the sweat and fear of yesterday – and she'd come back. She was walking up and down, smiling at men passing by, breasts poked forward. As if she had never been away.

Jack turned off the digger and ran out of the driveway.

'What are you doing back here?' he yelled at her.

He grabbed Katya by the arms to hold her still.

'Let go of me.' She shook him off. 'I am a working girl. This is my pitch.'

She began strolling up the road. The traffic was heavy, buses and cars choking the lanes, the air full of fumes. He followed her, keeping up as she turned back at the end of her pitch.

'You asked for my help,' he raged. 'You told me you had to get away or Johnny would kill you.'

'But you see, he didn't.' She thrust herself at him, heavily made up face and full bosom. 'See? I am not dead. He gave me medicine. Those stupid women know nothing. You know nothing. You chucked me in the back of your dirty van.'

'You asked me to get you away. I risked my life.'

'I am alive,' she said. 'I have my shoes again. I had medicine this morning. Those women, they put me in a house full of mothers with kids. All that racket and no medicine. They wouldn't listen to me.'

Jack could see it was pointless arguing. He wanted to hit her, but that would be worse than pointless. She was back, she had her shoes. Johnny must have given them to her. He couldn't hope that she hadn't told him about his own part in her brief escape. Why wouldn't she? She had no loyalty.

He left her, his head electric. What on earth was he going to do? Johnny would be after him. Johnny would kill him. It would be crazy just to wait here for him. He had to get away. No wasting time. Johnny knew where he was. He couldn't be a sitting duck.

Jack turned back, to confirm she was really out there. Not simply his fear. There she was, short skirt and red high heels, up and down the pavement, as if nothing had happened.

Owing him nothing at all.

He drove the digger back in and parked it out the way. Leaving the planks where they were, just grabbing his tools, he went to his van and ripped open the side door. He was putting the bench in, when Johnny came out of the hotel French windows. He at once saw Jack, beamed and strolled over as if about to shake his hand. Bobble hat on, he must have a wardrobe of them, long, dark grey coat. He was taking off his kid gloves.

'Nice morning, Jack.'

'It is,' he said. Waiting for the inevitable.

'You stole my woman, mate.' He punched a fist into his palm with a hard smack. 'Why did you do that?'

'She said she wanted to get away.'

'That's not your business, pal. She's my stable. I paid good money for her. She doesn't know what she wants. Back already, see. You're a fool. I told you yesterday. But then, I didn't realise how much of one you were, till Katya gave me the gen. It was you out at Epping. You sawing off the tag. You took her to some women.'

'They had a refuge place for her.'

'That's what you're going to need, pal.'

Johnny swung a punch, cracking Jack on the jaw. He fell back against the side of the van. And Johnny was on him, punching and kicking, kneeing, slapping and spitting in his excitement. Jack tried to hold him off, getting in the odd punch and kick, but Johnny was stronger and better practised.

'I can't let you go, Jack, even if I wanted to. You dirtbag! If they see me doing nothing when I'm wronged, they'll all be off. You're offal, mate.' He grabbed Jack by the hair and thumped him against the van. Once, twice.

Jack tried to push him away, feeling wetness in his hair, his body shaking with each smash against the metal sides. He was seeing double, pain in the guts and legs. His hand stretched into the van, felt the shaft of a claw hammer. He swung it wildly, into Johnny's face.

Johnny fell back, spitting out a tooth. Jack swung again and hit him on the side of the head. Johnny was staggering. Jack was about to hit again when he felt his arm gripped. He turned with the hammer high. There was Fi.

'Leave him, Jack.'

Jack let his hand drop. The hammer fell to the ground. Johnny had collapsed, lying flat out, gasping, blood seeping into his white bobble hat. His eyes were shut, his kid gloves lying on the ground by his feet.

'Self defence,' Jack managed to say. 'He attacked me.'

'I can't say that,' she exclaimed. 'It's Johnny. I can't say that. You must get away from here. He'll kill you.'

'He was killing me.'

'I can't say anything. I didn't see any of this. Go away. Run! I'm not here. I've seen nothing.'

She had backed off, her hands pressing him away. She turned and ran into the hotel.

Blood was softly bubbling out of Johnny's mouth. He was moaning. How alive was he? Dead enough to be lying down. Out of action. Jack knew he had to get away before he came to. He'd drive away, somewhere, anywhere. Miles away from here. Scotland. The Outer Hebrides. He staggered to the van. At the door, he realised he couldn't drive. He was seeing double, shaking.

He gave up on the van. He had to get away from here, and took the only form of transport he could manage. Jack got on to Betelgeuse. He didn't need the arm and the bucket, just its forward motion. All he needed to do was direct it. He drove through the arch, out the driveway and on to the pavement. He almost ran over Katya, who stepped aside just in time.

'You are a mad man!' she screamed.

Everyone was agreed on that. He had no counter argument as he drove the digger along the pavement. Cars in the road were hooting at his zigzag driving. Fortunately, top speed was four miles an hour, blood rolling down his face, soaking into his collar and shirt front. The world was a blur. He headed roughly ahead. Or where he thought was ahead.

He crossed several roads with Betelgeuse, shovel high and triumphant, the traffic hooting, pedestrians yelling as he scattered them. He ignored them all; they were in another world, having a go at someone else. Not Jack on the digger, getting away.

On their phones taking photos, shouting into them, pointing him out.

A dance to the music of pumping blood, added syncopation from car horns, lights flashing in his eyes. Away, drive. He headed across traffic lights, the colour of them not his concern, and bumped up the pavement. Johnny was after him. Johnny would kill him.

If Johnny was alive.

Jack stopped Betelgeuse. He staggered off. A man tried to hold him or help him, but Jack pushed him away and leaned his full weight against the swing doors. They opened and he almost fell into the foyer. The others, waiting, stared at the bloody, staggering man. He headed for the uniformed policeman behind the counter who had eyes only for him.

'Get me Fayyad!' he yelled. 'Detective Sergeant Fayyad Kamani!'

And collapsed.

Chapter 35

Jack opened his eyes, blinking in the light. Fayyad was wiping blood off his face. He attempted to tell his friend that Johnny would kill him if he caught him, repetitious and muddled, and interrupted when the paramedics came through the double doors.

Efficiently, Jack was stretchered into the ambulance which set off for the hospital, siren blaring. A uniformed officer accompanied him. The paramedic inside soothed him, telling him not to talk, that they'd be at Newham Hospital in five minutes, he'd be alright. She gave him tissues to hold to his bleeding head, changing them every few minutes.

At the hospital, over the next few hours, the bleeding was halted and he was questioned by doctors and nurses about what hurt where? About his blurred vision. His head was stitched in several places, X-rays were taken, and plasters applied here and there about his face and body.

The decision was made to keep him in; they wouldn't say for how long. The police constable tried for a single room, saying Jack's life could be in danger. But none were available. The best they could offer was a four person ward.

Jack was taken there in a wheelchair. He was sedated, and slept through the night and much of the next morning.

He awoke stiff and aching, but his eyes had recovered. He could barely lift his left arm, with his right he felt the stitches about his face and skull. A nurse came; she gave him some tablets and disconnected the drip. He was able to drink a little juice.

Someone had left fruit. He ate a few grapes, managed half a banana, and considered what he knew. Katya, Fi, Johnny, Malik, how they connected with Norma Jean. Trying to fit them together in a way that made sense. He had no reading material, and could not have concentrated if he had. He lay back, shifting every few minutes in a vain attempt to get comfortable with his aches and pains, ruminating. Fi's last words to him he went over again and again. Her refusal to help. Could it mean what he thought? Surely not. But only one tale made sense.

For lunch, he was able to eat a yogurt and the rest of the banana. He picked at the grapes. Mid afternoon Fayyad came with a bunch of daffodils. He sat down by the side of the bed.

'How you feeling, Jack?'

'I'm one big ache.'

'You certainly cleared the pavement on the Romford Road.'

Jack almost grinned, but winced at the pain in his jaw. 'That was crazy. But I had to get away from the hotel. I couldn't drive or walk. It was crazy going on the digger. I wasn't thinking straight. I'd hit Johnny with a hammer.'

'We know. He's in here. In a coma. We've got the hammer too.'

'He was trying to kill me.'

'Any witnesses?'

'There's Fi, Fi Morton, the cook and chambermaid. You met her the other day. You know, the actress. She saw it.'

'She said she didn't. We questioned her. She said she heard nothing. Told us she was vacuuming the rooms.'

'She's lying.'

'Why would she do that?'

'She's afraid of Johnny. He's got a hold on her.'

'What would that be?'

'The murder of Norma Jean.'

'Are you saying Fi killed her? Why? She doesn't even rate as a suspect.'

'I've been lying here the last couple of hours. Thinking of what I know, what I'd almost forgotten. It ties together, there's a few gaps. But you've got a murder, Fayyad.'

A doctor had come in. A short Asian woman wearing a white coat, a stethoscope round her neck.

'How are you feeling today, Mr Bell?'

'Very stiff. I'm aching all over.'

'No broken bones,' she said. 'Your head X-ray is fine. You're patched up. You look like Frankenstein's monster, but there's not a lot else we can do for you.'

'Can I go home?'

'You can, but no work,' she said, waving a stern finger. 'You need a couple of weeks' rest. Someone really bashed you about. There's been a policeman on duty outside the ward. Can you tell me why?'

'I'm Detective Sergeant Kamani,' said Fayyad. 'A cop and a friend. We feared Jack might be in danger, but that is less likely now.'

'We don't want him back here in a body bag,' said the doctor.

'I think he'll be OK.'

'Let's hope you're right, sergeant.' She turned to Jack. 'Take it easy, Mr Bell. Liquid food the next day or so. That doesn't mean booze.'

'I don't drink.'

'Very sensible. We deal with too many drink casualties here. Drunken drivers, their victims. Friday nights we are swamped with vomit from scantily dressed young women and aggressive young men. But enough from me on my bugbear.'

Jack could've added his own alcohol experiences, as he'd ended up in a number of hospitals with no clue how he'd got there. Instead, he thanked her.

'All in a day's work,' she said with a smile. 'I wish you well.' She passed on to the next bed.

'I can leave,' he said to Fayyad, sitting up, attempting to stretch his arms.

With some effort, he drew off the duvet. He was wearing hospital pyjamas, light, short, vaguely indecent. Fayyad had gone to the locker by the bed.

'Just the working clothes you came in,' he said. 'Oh, you can't wear this shirt and vest.' He held them up for Jack's inspection. They were covered in blood. 'I've a tracksuit in my car.'

'Get it for me,' said Jack. 'Please.'

Fayyad went off. While he was gone, Jack practised walking along the ward. He ambled like a man of ninety-nine, grasping the bed ends. The aches and pains down his body seemed to double his weight. He certainly couldn't work. How much did he have in the bank? What had happened to Betelgeuse? He needed to get the hired cement mixer back.

Some phone calls had to be made when he got home.

Fayyad returned with the tracksuit. Jack put it on, and put his bloody gear in a plastic bag. At the ward desk, he collected his phone, keys and money. And they left the hospital.

Chapter 36

Fayyad drove back to Forest Gate. Jack lay back in the passenger's seat, stretching out his legs. The skin on his head was drawn tight. Closing his eyes, he could pinpoint where Johnny had laid every punch. All aches and pains, but relieved to be leaving the hospital. He could rest up at home.

Fayyad said, 'So let's have your thoughts. You started to tell me when we got waylaid by the doctor. What have you worked out?'

'A fair bit,' said Jack. 'But there's holes still to fill. I need to know about Shenfield. Who is Norma Jean?'

'She is Anne McEwen. Married to Robert McEwen, better known to you and me as Noddy.'

'Noddy from Cumberland? Johnny's mate?' said Jack, surprised. 'Who'd believe that? All our school pals.'

'Not quite pals. Never that. But Noddy has made a success of himself. In his terms anyway. He has a palatial house in Shenfield with nasty dogs roaming the grounds. Essex Police know he's up to all sorts of dirty tricks but haven't been able to pin anything on him. As yet. He's worth a packet.'

'And beat his wife, Norma Jean. OK. I've got the gist. And she had a sister in Forest Gate?'

'Joy. She gave us the information that took us to Noddy McEwen.' He gave a short laugh. 'Noddy was all over us to begin with. So pleased to see someone from the old days. But he turned on us when we wouldn't give him full details. And kicked me and Hayley out, threatening to set the dogs on us.'

'He always had a short temper. I remember him at school, throwing a chair out of the window.'

'So we have Norma Jean or Anne, depending what name you prefer, from Shenfield. Though I think we should give her real name, Anne. Not the one Malik put in the book.'

'Abused by her husband, our school pal Noddy. He restricted her totally and beat her up.'

'Hang about, Jack. You know too much. We know Anne was bruised, but how are you so sure it was her husband's work?'

'He put an electronic tag on her. You didn't know that. Because it was taken off Anne, and ended up on Katya. What sort of husband puts an electronic tag on his wife?'

'How do you know Anne had a tag?'

'Katya told me.'

'How did she know?'

'We'll get to that,' said Jack. 'Let's start in Shenfield. Anne McEwen decided that she can't take her husband's punishment any longer. Maybe after a beating he'd given her. Maybe he's getting wind she wants to do a runner, so he put an electronic tag on her ankle which restricted her to the house and garden. She can't get it off as it has a combination lock. But she has to get away. She calls a taxi...'

'She didn't have a phone.'

'Used the house landline. The taxi comes. Her tag restricts her range to the house and grounds but there's bound to be overspill. Beyond the front garden, out in the street, Norma was still on the tag's home range. So she was able to go out the gate without the hue and cry. And then she's off in the taxi. That's when the tag starts bleeping. She's out of range, and the tag switches to a GPS signal. I suspect she didn't know that. A mean machine. The taxi takes her to Shenfield Station. There she gets a train to Forest Gate where her sister lives. The tag bleeps all along her route.'

'She probably chose a time when her husband and staff were busy,' mused Fayyad. 'A party maybe, with the staff busy, handing round drinks and snacks. So she'd have a head start. She's on the train, everyone's partying... Hang about.' He pulled to the side of the road and halted. 'I'm going to crash if I keep talking like this.' He put on the handbrake. 'Go on.'

'Anne doesn't know the GPS is following her all the way,' said Jack. 'She gets out at Forest Gate, but it's late at night. She thinks, she can't just turn up at her sister's house. So she goes to a local hotel, The Gate. She books in, she's got money I'm sure. Forget what Malik said. I'd guess she had a suitcase too with a few clothes and personal effects. Somewhere around about this time, her husband Noddy finds she's done a runner.'

'But he knows where she is from the GPS signals,' chimed in Fayyad. 'Exactly where she is. At The Gate Hotel. Now I see how the others fit in. Noddy contacts his old pal Johnny who works the area. He has girls in hotels along Romford Road.'

'Noddy tells Johnny to kill her.'

'Makes sense. I'm sure they've done lots together. So what happens next? You know the hotel better than me.'

'Malik books her into room 8 first. Remember? A single room. She's just a normal guest at that point. Then Johnny shows up, about midnight. I'm guessing Malik has worked with Johnny before. Helped him dispose of a girl or two. So the two of them plan a murder. There's money in it, Noddy being loaded. And it's made all the easier as Malik has a room set up.'

'Set up for what?'

'To kill his wife, Geela. Malik has had enough of her. She complains about his affairs, the way he runs the hotel. She talks about divorce all the time, they have screaming rows.

He wants rid of her. So he intends murdering her and marrying Fi.'

'Did Fi know of his plans?'

'If you'd asked me yesterday, I'd have punched you on the nose. She had me fooled. Making me breakfast, going out with me. But when I bashed Johnny, then she wants nothing to do with me. She saw him go for me plain as day. But she denies it.'

'Could be fear.'

'I don't think so. She's not continually stoned like Katya. She could at least have said she saw us fighting. Something to assist me.'

'She says she saw nothing. Why doesn't she want to help you?'

'That's what I kept thinking at the hospital. Johnny is in a coma. I could go down for it. Isn't that so?'

'You are certainly wanted for questioning.'

'And Fi's seen nothing. There can only be one reason.'

'Johnny is her partner in crime.'

'Dead right. Look at her situation. Fi is an unsuccessful actor. Can't get a paid acting job, so she's grubbing along in the hotel. But she's getting on in years, she can't keep pretending that the big break is round the corner. She has to find something else. Something with a future. And the hotel offers it. She's smart; she knows exactly how the place runs, knows how to make it into a decent, profitable place...'

'But not with Geela around.'

'Exactly. Fi set her cap on Malik. And he's game. Wife number one is getting old, losing her looks, hates the hotel. Malik wants rid of her. He and Fi set up room 6 to kill Geela, one night when she's staying over at the hotel. But in the meantime, Norma Jean, I mean Anne, shows up. And maybe 30 minutes later Johnny Potter comes along saying there's money to be made if Malik assists in the murder of Anne. Malik is eager and probably Fi too. My guess is she was staying with him that night. So why not give the plan they'd set up for Geela a rehearsal? Anne is taken out of room 8 and given room 6. Either willingly or forcibly. I'm guessing forcibly with Johnny around. Then they have a party. Johnny, Malik, Fi, Katya invited to make the numbers up, with Anne McEwen as the unwilling guest.'

'Out of it on GHB, a date rape drug, most likely,' said Fayyad. 'It breaks down rapidly so won't show up in any lab report.'

'That night, Anne is more out of it than in. They drink and make merry with each other, swap partners, and so forth. That's when Katya saw Anne had a tag on her ankle.'

'I follow you so far,' said Fayyad. 'It makes sense up to then. But the party is over. Everyone leaves but the murderer. Let's think about this. How does he kill her? Must inject a poison to simulate heart attack. Injected somewhere the needle point won't be seen, the armpit or groin. I take that. But the door is locked from the inside. How does the murderer get out?'

'Let's go to the hotel.'

Chapter 37

They parked at the back of the hotel. Jack was dismayed the side door of his van was open, exactly how he'd left it when Johnny appeared yesterday morning. He looked inside, hoping nothing had been taken.

'Can't see anything gone. Have to check.'

'You're not here to take an inventory, Jack. Besides which, you're not going to be working for a few weeks.'

Jack locked the van. He crossed fingers nothing valuable had gone.

They crossed the car park to his workings. The planks were there, ready to be made up as forms, as he'd left them. The cement sacks were out of the way, covered in a plastic sheet. The bags were thick; they'd be OK till he got back to work. The cement mixer, intended to be working non-stop yesterday, was alongside, its gaping mouth screaming its neglect. It had to be returned as he'd hired it by the day. A waste of cash to keep it here idle. He'd hire it again when he was fit.

Jack considered the lengths of form wood. They'd probably be OK as forms were only temporary, to be taken out once the cement was hardening. Best cover them. Who knows how long he'd be out of action. Money though. He had to live. No work, no cash. He must have a good look at his bank account, see how much, what he owed, who could be held off for how long. It would be tight.

'You OK, Jack?'

'This is depressing.' He had an awful thought. 'What's happened to Betelgeuse?'

'Who?'

'My digger.'

'Weird name you've got for it. It's a star isn't it?'

'Yes, a red giant in Orion. Where's my digger?'

'Don't worry. It's in the police station car park. I was going to tell you about that; the boss says it has to go.'

'I'll get Bob to pick it up tomorrow. Let's go inside, before I think of anything else I have to do.'

They went through the French windows into the hotel. Geela was at the desk. She stared at Jack aghast.

'I heard you'd been in the wars,' she said, her hands to her face. 'Johnny really smashed you up. But no one will tell me why.'

'I tried to help Katya get away from him.'

Geela pursed her lips. 'Oh, he wouldn't like that. He doesn't let her do anything, except go out on the street. He's got a temper, that man.' She leaned forward, looking about her. 'Where is he? Katya is going crazy for him.'

'In hospital,' said Fayyad.

'May he never come out again,' said Geela vehemently. 'He is a nasty, bullying man. Malik and him do some things together. I don't ask. Can't be good. Maybe you should investigate.'

'We are,' said Fayyad. 'Can we have the key to room 6?'

'What for? The room has been cleaned several times since the woman was taken away.'

'Oh, just an idea I've got,' said Jack.

She shrugged and opened the key drawer.

'And can we have the office key too?' said Jack.

'You think Malik is cooking the books?' She chuckled. 'You are most welcome to have a good look. Just don't shut us down.'

She handed over the keys to Fayyad. He thanked her and bounded up the stairs. Jack plodded behind him, foot after heavy foot, pulling himself up the banisters. So few steps, so much effort.

Once in the upstairs hallway, he leaned against the wall to catch his breath.

'You OK, Jack?'

'I feel like an arthritic lobster,' he said. 'But at least I'm up and about, which is more than can be said for Johnny.'

'I'll do what I can,' said Fayyad. He put an arm on Jack's shoulder. 'But I must tell you, it's being considered whether to charge you.'

'He attacked me,' exclaimed Jack. 'I was defending myself.'

'No witnesses.'

'Except Fi. Who saw nothing.'

'If it comes to court,' said Fayyad, 'you'd have a good case for self defence. Johnny has a record of violence.'

'I can prove that I helped Katya which is why Johnny went for me. I drove her to Epping Forest and sawed the tag off her ankle. I bet we can find the sawn off tag in the forest. Along with my Faraday cage.'

'What on earth is a Faraday cage?'

'It's a device made of mesh that cuts off electronic signals, in this case from the tag, so I could get Katya away without Johnny knowing. I took her to my ex wife, Alison. She'll be my witness. She fixed up a refuge for Katya. But instead of staying, the stupid cow came back. Johnny keeps her bunged up with drugs. She told him who helped her get away and Johnny came for me. He would have killed me if I hadn't grabbed a hammer.'

'Johnny may not want to press charges,' Fayyad mused. 'That's if he wakes up.'

'I'm not going to be praying by his bedside.'

'From what you say, you have a good case. I'd guess it won't get to court. Johnny doesn't gather much sympathy. You'll be OK.'

Fayyad lightly punched Jack on the shoulder. Jack winced.

'Sorry, mate. Let's look at the room.' He turned to put the key in the lock.

'Hang on, Fayyad. Before we go in, let's go back three days. Monday, when I still had legs that worked. Malik asked me to come up with a plan to divide room 6 in two. So he brought me up here. We found the door locked with the key on the inside. I went back down, got a hammer, screwdriver and a six inch nail. By the time I'd come back up, Fi had joined Malik. They wanted me here. Needed me.'

'As a witness,' said Fayyad. 'They both knew Anne McEwen was dead in the room, but needed you to corroborate that the room was locked from the inside.'

'Malik doesn't want to divide the room in two. It was just his ruse to get me up here. To be their witness. Not once has he asked me for the estimate for the work. And if I gave it to him, bet your bottom dollar he'd say too expensive, or maybe next year – or never.'

'So you knocked the key through,' said Fayyad.

'I did.'

'A perfect witness. Let's go inside. Following your footsteps.'

Fayyad opened the door of room 6. It was bright and airy, the bed made, the curtains open revealing the traffic of Romford Road and the pale grey sky of a wintry afternoon.

'It's had a total clean up,' said Fayyad looking about him.

'The room's been occupied a few times since Monday,' said Jack. 'They're not sentimental in the hotel trade.'

'So what are we looking for?' Fayyad was going around the walls. They were white and bare, his fingers brushing lightly along. 'No doors I can see,' he said, 'except this one.' He was standing by the room door.

'Switch on the light,' said Jack.

Fayyad flipped the switch. Nothing happened.

'It's not working,' he said.

'It hasn't been working since I've been here,' said Jack.

'Is that important?'

'Bring in the ladder. Just up the hallway where I left it. I would get it, except I can't lift a matchbox.'

Fayyad went out. Jack rested on the arm of the sofa. He hated being so useless, but he'd better get used to it. As soon as he got home, he'd have the longest soak in the bath. Spend two weeks in it.

Fayyad returned with the step ladder.

'Now what?'

'Set it up under the light. And have a close look.'

Fayyad set up the ladder. He took off his jacket, brushed it down and laid it over the back of the sofa. His shirt was gleaming white against his brick red tie.

Fayyad climbed the step ladder. The bulb was in a paper shade. He looked up at the ceiling in puzzlement, then turned to Jack.

'What am I looking for?'

'Go up two more steps.'

'I'm no mountain climber,' he said, cautiously taking another step, then another, standing shakily near the top of the ladder. 'Now what? Before I come tumbling down.'

'Push the ceiling,' said Jack.

Above Fayyad's head was the ceiling rose, a circle about two feet across, the circumference an intertwined floral pattern, surrounding the hanging light. Fayyad gave a small push, worried that he might propel himself off the steps.

'Harder,' said Jack.

Fayyad gave a fierce thrust. And the circle of ceiling lifted several inches. Shaken by his effort, he took a step down and gripped the ladder. The indented circle of ceiling glared at them.

'Feel the ceiling rose,' said Jack.

Fayyad tentatively took a step up again and pushed his fingers at the rose. 'It's rubbery,' he said. 'Not plaster.'

'Ceiling roses are brittle usually. Not intended to be manhandled,' said Jack. 'Let's go upstairs.'

Chapter 38

Jack made his way laboriously to the top floor. The stairs in his own flat were going to be a daily chore. But at least he was moving, unlike Johnny.

Fayyad was waiting on the landing. Jack leaned against the wall, looking down the stairs. At least gravity would be working with him going down.

Once he'd caught his breath, he said, 'That room is Malik's office. Let's go in.'

Fayyad opened the door with the key that Geela had given him. There was barely room for the two of them inside with the filing cabinets, shelving and the desk piled with papers. Pushed into the eaves were boxes, files and assorted oddments.

'He's quite a squirrel, Malik,' said Fayyad. He indicated the folded camp bed with the bedding alongside. 'I don't blame Geela for not wanting to sleep up here.'

Jack sat in a chair. He was looking at the floor.

'It's an attic space,' said Fayyad looking around him. 'Once things get up here they never come down.'

'Would you move those boxes?' said Jack. 'I'm useless.'

Two cardboard boxes were on a rug. Fayyad lifted one of them, needing to get both hands under it, as it was packed full of papers.

'It's tricky finding somewhere to put it down.'

He settled for the desk, papers and ledgers under it. The second box went on top of the first.

Jack pulled away the rumpled rug. They stared at what was at once obvious. A circle of floor was raised a few inches.

'So the office is above room 6,' said Fayyad. 'That's what I pushed up.'

He got down on his knees. In the centre of the circle was a hinged handle lying flat. Fayyad raised the handle, put his hand through and pulled. Slowly a tube of floor rose as he tugged. It was like a bird cage with broomstick size poles, connecting the top to a circle of ceiling, along with the light and its shade.

'The light that doesn't work,' said Jack.

Fayyad drew out the cylinder and laid it on the floor. On all fours, he gazed down the hole. He could see an area of carpet and some of the bed.

'You'd need to be slim to get down there,' he said. 'Not sure I could.'

'Fi's slim,' said Jack. 'So's Malik for that matter.'

Fayyad sat up, looking at the circular birdcage and the hole in the floor.

'There needs to be a rope or something,' he said, 'to get up and down.'

'A rope ladder,' said Jack. 'Over there.' He pointed it out. 'Malik says it's in case of fire.'

Fayyad crossed to where Jack was pointing. He brought back the roll of rope ladder.

'Just the right width,' he said, trying the ladder across the hole in the floor.

'Made to measure,' said Jack.

'Where would it be attached?' Fayyad pondered, searching close by. 'Ah. These screw holes in the desk side. Must be. They'd hold it. What do you think, Jack?'

'Yep. I reckon hooks go in there. They'd hold the dowel at the top of the ladder. Probably find them somewhere. In one of the drawers, I expect.'

Fayyad was looking at the birdcage, turning it round.

'You'd need to be a good carpenter to make that.'

'Fi was a stage manager at one time. And pretty good with tools, she told me. The rubber ceiling rose, I bet she learnt that in a theatre somewhere.'

'A pity she doesn't make better use of her skills.'

'Malik pushed her to go out with me,' said Jack. 'I was surprised. First time I'd met her. I've been thinking about that. Why would he set me up with his girl?' He sighed, thinking of his relationship with Fi.

'He was planning ahead,' said Fayyad.

'That's what I think. Fi was going to be my girlfriend for a while, just long enough to allay suspicion. In a few months, they'd murder Geela. Make it look like a heart attack. Malik is a respectable married man, grieving. Not someone with a girlfriend eager to step into his wife's shoes.'

'And when the fuss dies down,' said Fayyad, 'she lives happily ever after with Malik.' Fayyad sighed. 'Good tale. But evidence, Jack, as my boss will say.' He looked about the room. 'I wonder if there's anything else here.'

'Might well be. They'd have to dispose of Anne's suitcase, clothes and ID,' said Jack. 'Could be bits and pieces piled under this lot. Malik is pretty tight. He wouldn't want to throw out anything that he could sell. He ground me down to the last penny on my contract.'

'This room will stay locked,' said Fayyad rising to his feet. 'Room 6 too. I have to talk to my boss. Get the crime scene people back.' He pressed his fingers together. 'I wonder how they'll react under questioning. Fi and Malik. Stay shtum. Or both blame the other? Have to question Katya for whatever that's worth. Maybe Johnny will wake up. I doubt we'll get anything on Anne's husband. He's in Shenfield and well practised at keeping his distance.'

Fayyad opened the door of the office. 'I'm going to get you home, Jack. And then go straight to the station. We more or less know what's what. All we have to do is prove it.'

Chapter 39

Jack was soaking in the bath, laid out flat in water as hot as he could stand it. His radio was on. Some of the songs were annoying but it was too much effort for him to reach the chair it was on with his soapy fingers. It was as much as he could do to keep the hot water topping up.

He had his best thoughts in the bath.

The light that didn't work. Something so easy to fix if it was a loose connection. But no, they didn't want extra wire getting in the way of their cylinder of floor and ceiling. It had to come out neatly. Clever, the rubber ceiling rose. He imagined Fi climbing up the rope ladder like a pirate, with the hypodermic in her teeth. Then handing it to Malik above, and down she'd go to get the other bits and pieces belonging to the dead woman. A small suitcase might just poke through, or maybe Malik had taken that out with him when he left through the door. A little drunk, the whole party. If sober they might just have left everything, and not created suspicion at a woman dying in a room without ID, luggage or money.

Or maybe that was Noddy's directive. Hoping she'd die and be buried without being identified. Instead it had bothered Fayyad. Johnny then had made a mistake with the tag. Noddy must have given him the code to take it off Anne's ankle. Johnny thought, why waste it, and put it on Katya, which set that whole episode in train involving Jack.

Fi had used him. At least he'd got breakfast and coffee out of her. Seen the most boring play in the universe. He would never forget those wasted hours at the King's Head. They'd only gone out that once. She'd backed out of coming on Wanstead Flats for a night of stargazing. He didn't believe she'd gone to see her sick mother. Most likely she was spending the night with Malik.

She had to keep Malik sweet. A key part of her plan. Geela would be murdered in a couple of months. But Malik couldn't remarry straight away. Geela would be cremated. Any possible evidence of poisoning gone in the fire. The hole in the ceiling and its birdcage plug would be erased. Fi would do it. Not the most difficult of jobs, and her carpentry was good.

A lot of supposition. Bits of evidence, here and there. Searching the office might recover more. He had dismissed Geela's accusations against Fi. But Geela was right. Her husband was sleeping with Fi. Geela might have evidence and would be willing to give it, once she was told what the lovers were planning.

And Johnny in his coma. Long may that last.

An announcement of the time on the radio slapped Jack, and had him leaping out of the bath in spite of the pain.

Still naked, he phoned a taxi. Half wet, he dressed, the exertions painful. He gave up trying to put socks on, his feet were too far down his body. Jack was still dressing when his doorbell rang. He slipped on his trainers without doing up his laces. He'd suffer cold feet. And he headed downstairs, his jacket, scarf and woolly hat in hand, stumbling down the steps. The taxi driver would know he was coming, might wonder how many there were, with his heavy footfall. Jack opened the door to an Asian man in a turban.

'Taxi to Sarah Bonnell school?'

'That's me,' said Jack.

He followed the man down the path, still clutching his outdoor clothing. On the pavement, the man turned.

He said, 'Stay there. I'll drive closer.'

'Thank you.'

While waiting, Jack put on his jacket and scarf, stuffing the hat in the pocket. He was twenty minutes late for Mia's concert. He'd been lounging in the bath, keeping the hot water going, ruminating. He could have easily been on time with just a wash. But he'd simply forgotten about the concert after the hotel discoveries.

The drive took five minutes. Arriving at the school, he overpaid the taxi driver and lumbered to the entrance. The glass door was stiff. A girl in uniform opened it for him. She stared at him as if he'd come to the wrong place.

'I'm here for the concert,' he said.

She put a finger to her lips. 'Sh! It's in progress.'

Jack nodded. Another girl at a table asked for his name. When he gave it, she went down the list on her sheets and crossed him off.

'Your wife is already here,' she said.

He didn't correct her on his relationship with Alison.

'Please go in quietly.'

Another girl led him to some double doors. She opened one and he slipped in. The audience were in semi darkness, lights were directed onto the stage where a girls' choir was singing a song about a broken hearted maiden in the valley below. In front of the stage, at ground level, a teacher was conducting them. Although resting against the wall, he needed to sit down. Somewhere in the audience would be Alison with presumably a seat for him. He slipped down to the floor. He'd get up when this lot had finished.

Had he missed Mia's quartet? It would be ironic if, with all this fuss and flurry, he had. He must get a walking stick. The charity shop up the road would have one. The ground was so far down.

The choir sang two more songs. Then stopped. There was applause. Jack rose to see them leaving the stage. He walked slowly down the mid aisle seeking out Alison; he couldn't see too well in the half light. Chairs were being put out on the stage and music stands.

'Jack!'

He turned in the direction of the hissed call. And saw Alison waving, mid row. He eased his way through the people, excuse me, excuse me, until he arrived at the empty seat beside her.

'You're very late,' she said crossly. 'You missed her first set. Fortunately, they've got another.' She peered at his face. 'You look dreadful.'

'I got beaten up,' he said.

'Quite badly. May I ask why?'

'Katya's minder was upset with me.'

'Ah,' said Alison. 'You know she didn't stay at the refuge?'

'She came back. Would you believe it? And ratted on me,' said Jack. 'He would have killed me.'

'What did you do to him?'

'Hit him with a hammer.'

Alison sucked in a breath. 'Normally, I don't approve of violence, but I can make an exception. Do you need a lift home?'

'Yes, I do.'

'I'm sure we can manage that. At least you're here. Mia is in this orchestra too. Sh, sh. They're almost ready.'

On stage, girls were sitting down with various instruments. At one side, there was Mia with two other cello players.

Jack was too uncomfortable to enjoy the music of the school orchestra. He shuffled in the seat until told by a man behind to stop moving about. He gritted his teeth, his legs needed to stretch, his body to lie out flat. He was solid ache, every muscle and bone.

Jack endured, having no idea whether the music was any good or not. He was barely listening, the sound of his aches drowning it out. The orchestra left the stage. A gospel choir of mostly black girls came on. They might've been good. They might not have been. They were followed by a string quartet, including Mia and her cello.

Jack closed his eyes. Music was playing but his legs were screaming, his back itching. They played two pieces. He applauded, because everyone else was.

'Good, weren't they?' said Alison.

'Yes.'

The choir returned for a couple of pop numbers. Then final applause. Thank goodness, thought Jack. All the players crowded onto the stage. They bowed three times in unison. The applause went on for a minute or two, petered out and the girls left the stage. The lights came up in the auditorium.

Jack hobbled out of the row, at least he could stretch his legs. His back was so itchy. Alison followed him as he scratched his lower back. Mia was waiting at the end of the row.

She looked at him aghast. 'You're a disgrace, Dad. The girls at the door said this dreadful man came in late. I didn't realise it was you. Have you been drinking again?'

'How dare you!' exclaimed Alison. 'Your father has been beaten up trying to save a woman who was enslaved. In spite of that, he has come to your concert.'

'Sorry,' said Mia, hanging her head, her eyes filling at her mother's tirade. 'I didn't know, Dad. Sorry. Did you save the woman?'

'No,' he said. 'I tried though.'

'Thank you for coming,' she said, gripping his hand. 'Did you enjoy our set?'

'It was wonderful,' he said. 'Wonderful.'

Chapter 40

Three Weeks Later

The form wood had survived. He had meant to cover them up, but though it had bothered him, stumbling about with his walking stick had deterred any action. Dumb really, would it have been so difficult? But the weather had been kind while he'd been recovering. Cold, but dry. The sacks of cement were fine. And he wasn't too bad himself, all considered. It had been over a week before he could do a proper walk, even with a walking stick. At the end of two weeks, he'd given up the stick and was able to walk two miles to Stratford and back. He was more or less all there, and needed to earn money.

He'd rehired the cement mixer. He would put the forms in place and get on with laying the concrete.

Geela came out through the French windows. She was wearing a blue shalwar kameez and matching hijab.

'How are you, Jack?' She gripped his arm. 'Last time I saw you, you were like an old man.'

'I felt like one too. I'm a lot better. Taking it easy, I can still get this finished in a couple of days. Any chance of prompt payment?'

'Soon as you finish. But don't kill yourself,' she said with a half laugh. 'Enough of that already here. Oh, you missed all the excitement. The police came, a big mob. They shut room 6 and the office. They were taking things away in plastic bags. They arrested Malik and Fi. I knew they were sleeping together. I smelt it on his clothes, on her too. He says no, no, Geela. The lying bastard.' She leaned forward and said quietly, 'They were planning to kill me. Fi and Malik. Kill me and get married. I know you know. Detective Sergeant Kamani told me that you worked it out.'

'I gave him some help,' he said. 'A builder's eye. Told him why the light didn't work in room 6.'

'And that woman, Norma Jean, didn't have a heart attack. She was murdered. By Malik and Fi. Both in custody. The trial won't be for six months. I never want to see Malik again. I'm divorcing him. It's not good in our culture, but when your husband plans to murder you, what choice do you have?'

'How are you managing the cooking and cleaning the rooms?' With Fi gone, he thought, but didn't say.

'I'm employing two women.' She shrugged. 'They are OK. One cooks, the other is the chambermaid. Fi was a hard worker, but that's all you can say for her. She wanted to replace me. A schemer. I can make the hotel a better place. No more prostitutes and druggies.'

'Katya has gone?'

'I don't know where she is. I don't care.' She flapped her hands as if to get rid of a bad smell. 'The police spent a lot of time talking to her. I don't know what sense they got out of her. She doesn't like police. Not at all.' She giggled at the thought. 'And I haven't seen Johnny since you were here. Not that I am missing him.'

'He's still in a coma.'

'Best place for him.'

And so long as he was in a coma, Noddy McEwen was off the hook. Even if Johnny woke up, Fayyad said, and was prepared to accuse Norma's husband, he'd get the best lawyers in town to double-barrel Johnny's doubtful reputation.

She touched him on the shoulder. 'It's good to see you again, Jack. I'm pleased you're OK.'

'I need to earn money. Three weeks off work, I can't afford any longer.'

'Finish the work and I'll pay you straight away.' She looked in through the French windows. 'I must help in the kitchen. The new woman is slow. She'd better speed up soon, or I'll have to get rid of her.'

'You seem to have taken over at a run.'

'It's my place now,' she said. 'Not Malik's any more with his women and parties. I shall run it properly. My father is coming down to look at the books. We must get them straight. You want breakfast?'

'Yes, please.'

'I shall feed you up. Get you strong again.' She shook her hands to express her vibrancy. 'I've got plans for this place, Jack. The walls are too thin. You don't want to hear someone next door dropping a comb. The whole place needs decorating. You interested?'

'Of course.'

'We'll talk about it over breakfast.'

Geela went inside. Jack was impressed at her new energy. No longer chained to Malik.

And there was more work on the cards.

One job at a time, though you always had to look ahead. He wouldn't start laying concrete until breakfast was over, but he would get the form wood in place ready for it. Jack took a plank out of the bundle and laid it out. He looked in his notebook. The measurements he'd taken, before he'd been battered black and blue, still made sense. The plank had been marked up. All set.

He went to his van for the saw and bench.

Thank you!

I am grateful to every reader who finishes one of my novels. I have taken you on a journey which I hope you have enjoyed. There are plenty of things you could have been doing, other than reading this book. So, thank you for your time.

If you liked Jack At The Gate, here's what you can do next:

I'd appreciate a review on Amazon. In that way, you can help me tell other readers about my books. Without reviews authors get few sales on Amazon. So I'd be grateful for your review to help this series get on the move.

You can get a FREE ebook of Jack of Spades if you sign up for my readers' list. You may give it to a friend if you wish. Every month a lucky reader from the list will be sent a free, signed paperback of their choice from the series. Sign up using this link:

http://eepurl.com/buAh5H

When you sign up for my readers' list you will receive my regular newsletter. This will give you news about me, what I'm reading, tell you about my future books, PLUS a variety of giveaways.

Books by DH Smith

DH Smith is the name I use for my Jack of All Trades series. The books are all standalone novels and can be read in any order.

Out Now:
- Jack of All Trades
- Jack of Spades
- Jack o'Lantern
- Jack By The Hedge
- Jack In The Box
- Jack On The Tower
- Jack Recalled
- Jack at Death's Door
- Jack at the Gate

Books by Derek Smith

All my books, other than the Jack of All Trades series, are written under the name Derek Smith.

Mystery/Crime
Murder at Any Price

Fantasy
Hell's Chimney
The Prince's Shadow
Elektra

Other
Strikers of Hanbury Street (short stories)
Catching Up (poetry)

Young Adult Novels
Hard Cash
Half a Bike
Fast Food
Frances Fairweather Demon Striker!

Children's Novels
The Good Wolf
Feather Brains
Baker's Boy

For Younger Children
The Magical World of Lucy-Anne
Lucy-Anne's Changing Ways
Jack's Bus

About the Author

I live in Forest Gate in the East End of London. In my working life, I have been a plastics chemist, a gardener and a stage manager before becoming a professional writer. I began with plays, working with several theatre companies, and had a few plays on radio and TV, as well as on the stage. In the early 80s I became involved in running a co-operative bookshop and vegetarian café in Stratford, learning to cook, and having my first go at writing a novel. The first was a mess, and, after too many rewrites, binned. The transition from drama to novels took me a couple of years to get to grips with. My first success was a young adult novel, Hard Cash, published by Faber. Buoyed up by this, I stuck with children's work, did school visits, and made a hand to mouth living as a full time author, topped up with some evening class work in creative writing at City University and the Mary Ward Centre in Holborn. A few adult fiction titles appeared from time to time, between the children's list, and I have since been working more in that direction with my Jack of All Trades series.

My full name is Derek Howard Smith. I write as DH Smith for my Jack of All Trades series; all other books appear under Derek Smith. Earlham Books is my own imprint.

www.dereksmithwriter.com

The book you're holding was designed by Lia at Free Your Words...
Contact lia@freeyourwords.com for a quote

www.ingramcontent.com/pod-product-compliance
Lightning Source LLC
Chambersburg PA
CBHW061324200626
46813CB00017B/2838